WARS™

THE CLONE WARS™

DECIDE
YOUR
DESTINY

Written by Jonathan Green

Published by Ladybird Books Ltd 2010
A Penguin Company

Penguin Books Ltd, 80 Strand,
London, WC2R ORL, UK
Penguin Books Australia Ltd,
Camberwell, Victoria, Australia
Penguin Group (NZ), 67 Apollo Drive, Rosedale,
North Shore 0632, New Zealand
(a division of Pearson New Zealand Ltd)

www.ladybird.com

ISBN: 9781409390077

10 9 8 7 6 5 4 3 2 1

Printed in Great Britain

STAR WARS™

THE CLONE WARS™

DECIDE YOUR DESTINY

Crisis on Coruscant

How To Use Your Decide Your Destiny Book

Follow the instructions below before reading this book.

1. Go to: www.starwars.com/decideyourdestiny
2. Click 'Begin' to launch the book selection screen.
3. After selecting your book, the scene selection menu will appear.
4. Start reading the story on page 7 of this book and follow the instructions at the end of each section.
5. When you make a decision that takes you online, select the correct box and enter the corresponding code word as prompted.
6. After watching the scene or completing your online activity, return to the scene selection screen and continue your story.

Now turn the page and begin your adventure!

Crisis on Coruscant

START

You have only been in the service of Jedi Master Shaak Ti for a few weeks but you have already learnt as much as the Togruta's Padawan learner as you ever did at the Temple. The two of you – Master and apprentice – are currently tasked with serving as Senator Padmé Amidala of Naboo's personal bodyguard, after a series of death threats have been made against her.

Having just disembarked from the shuttle craft that has transported the Senator from her personal apartments, she and Master Ti are now deep in discussion about how to keep her safe, while she remains here on the Galactic Capital of Coruscant.

"We must take these threats against your life seriously, Senator," Shaak Ti says, "but you need not worry unnecessarily. As well as Commander Fox, my Padawan is also sworn to protect you."

"You would entrust my life to a Padawan?" the Senator asks, looking you up and down.

"I can assure you, Senator, that my Padawan is more than up to the task," Master Ti says. "And besides, it is not only my Padawan who will be protecting you. I shall also act as your personal bodyguard for as long as you remain here on Coruscant."

A clone trooper breaks away from the accompanying squad and approaches, the maroon markings on his armour denoting that he is one of the elite Coruscant Guard.

"General!" Commander Fox interrupts, throwing Master Ti a salute.

"What is it, Commander?"

"It would appear that the attack you were expecting has come."

"What attack? What's happening?" Padmé asks, trying to hide her anxiety.

"Senator Amidala, it would appear that it is not only your life that is in danger," Shaak Ti announces, her tone as placid and serene as ever. "The Senate itself is under attack. Quick, come with me."

"What?" the Senator says in disbelief. "I see no danger."

"There, ma'am!" Commander Fox says, lowering his electrobinoculars and pointing at the sky.

Everyone looks. The threat to the Senate's survival is just about visible to the naked eye, a dirty black speck against the crystal clear blue sky.

"Is that a spaceship?" Senator Amidala asks.

"It's a Trandoshan freighter," Commander Fox confirms, a few hand signals sending his clone troopers into the Senate building itself to get the Senators, and everyone else, out, "and it's heading this way."

"Can it be shot down?" Shaak Ti asks, remaining calm in spite of the Commander's dramatic revelation.

"Regrettably not without great loss of life elsewhere," Commander Fox points out. "The Senate must be evacuated!"

It is then that Master Ti turns to you. "It is my duty to ensure Senator Amidala's safety," she tells you. "I will remain with her and make sure that she gets away safely."

"What do you want me to do, Master?" you ask.

"Enter the Senate building. Find Chancellor Palpatine and ensure that he makes it to safety too."

Master Ti has entrusted you with a vital mission and the chance to prove yourself to her. But perhaps there is a way you could save the Chancellor and the Senate at the same time.

If you want to enter the Senate as instructed by Master Ti, turn to page 130.

If you want to suggest another way to save the Senate and the Chancellor, turn to page 41.

10 On Commander Fox's signal, the clone troopers storm the building, with you bringing up the rear. You enter the hangar in time to see the clones flush the haulage business's owner out of hiding. The blue-skinned Toydarian hovers in the air at the centre of a circle of Coruscant Guard troopers. Their guns are trained on the nervous-looking alien and his trunk-nose twitches fitfully.

And then, a split second later, you are throwing yourself to the floor as laser-fire rips through the building. Searing laser blasts shatter windows and a few rebound from the armour worn by the clones. You are sheltered from the deadly fusillade by a large heat shield panel. The Toydarian Commander Fox had cornered isn't so lucky. The alien drops to the floor of the hangar and doesn't move again.

As the laser-fire subsides, you glance over the top of the heat shield in time to see a hovering ASN-class droid quickly moving away from the scene of the Toydarian's murder. Someone sent that droid to silence the alien and stop your only lead from revealing what you need to know. The only way to find out who that was, and still have a chance of getting to the bottom of this mystery, is to follow that droid as it is recalled by its master.

As the clone troopers are only just beginning to recover from the unexpected attack, you are already on your feet and sprinting out of the hangar after the assassin droid.

Turn to page 56.

11 You acquitted yourself well during the attack on the Republic Senate and Shaak Ti is not one to withhold praise where praise is due.

"Well done, my Padawan," she says. "By your actions today, you have proved yourself a worthy apprentice. But although the threat has been averted for the time being, until we know who acted so ruthlessly against the Senate, the crisis on Coruscant will not be over."

"Who do you think was responsible, Master?" you ask.

"I cannot be certain, but I feel that Count Dooku and the Separatists had a hand in it." Shaak Ti fixes you with a grim expression. "But hunches and suppositions are not enough; what we need is proof."

"And where do we start looking for that?"

"We need to find out who chartered that freighter and set it on its collision course with the Senate. However, my immediate responsibilities lie with Senator Amidala. You as my Padawan, on the other hand . . ."

She lets the thought hang in the air between you.

You can hardly believe what she is implying. Your chest swells with pride. "You mean . . .?"

"I want you to head up the investigation. I know that Commander Fox is keen to pursue his own methods in the Underlevels – a 'shakedown' he called it. But as a native of Coruscant, perhaps you have other contacts you could bring into play. What say you? Will you accept this mission?"

"Of course," you tell Master Ti, feeling fit to burst with excitement. But how do you want to pursue your investigation?

If you want to join Commander Fox and the Coruscant Guard as they carry out their shakedown operation in the Underlevels of the planet-city, turn to page 23.

If you want to pursue the investigation more subtly on your own, calling on your contacts in the Upper City, turn to page 103.

13   "OK, we go after the smugglers," Commander Fox confirms with apparent satisfaction. "He's not going to get away this time."

The gunships peel off, cutting short their pursuit of the bounty hunter, and bear down on the smugglers' ship instead.

In no time at all, the more powerful LAAT/is have caught up with the freighter. The smugglers immediately deploy countermeasures, firing a fusillade of rockets, but the wing-mounted gunners take the missiles out before they can hit either gunship. Commander Fox has no choice but to order his men to return fire.

The freighter goes into terminal freefall as it crashes down in flames. You have stopped the Pacithhip smuggler gang and made the world-city just a slightly better place, and there may still be time to catch up with the fleeing Vogg Barakk.

Turn to page 54.

14 Leaping from platform to platform, you descend through the Senate Chamber to the bottom and from there make your way to the holding office beneath. But this too is deserted.

It can only be mere moments before the freighter hits the Senate now and you may not have enough time to make it to safety yourself, let alone rescue Chancellor Palpatine – but try you must!

Exiting the holding office as quickly as you can, you run into one of the Chancellor's personal Red Guard.

"Where is the Chancellor?" you demand, looking up into the faceless crimson mask of the sentry.

"The Chancellor has already left the building. He is safe," the Red Guard says gruffly. "And it's time we were out of here too. Now move!"

Turn to page 127.

15 The Jawas haul your battered landspeeder into the already packed hold of their sandcrawler, leaving you to find a comfortable niche for yourself, next to an open ventilation hatch and out of the way of the bickering scavengers. There you sit back to wait out the journey across the Great Mesa Plateau to Jabba's palace.

At suns-rise, you stir and open your eyes, having dozed off as the sandcrawler ground its way through the canyons of the desert wilderness. The first thing you see through the open hatch beside you is the ominous silhouette of Jabba the Hutt's palace, as it rises from the desert uplands like an island amidst the ochre sea of sand that surrounds it.

The Jawas have upheld their end of the bargain, but it's now up to you to decide how you want to approach the palace. Through a combination of sign language and urgent chirruping the Jawas inform you that they have their own secret way into the palace. The tunnel begins in one wall of the junkyard that lies behind the palace and that they call home.

If you want to make use of the Jawas' secret tunnel to enter the palace, turn to page 119.

If you want to approach the main gate instead and request an audience with the mighty Jabba, turn to page 144.

16 As dusk falls on the surface – the garish lights of the advertising billboards and air traffic signs coming on – you hail an air taxi and travel to the dark underbelly of the world-city, where night has already fallen in the shadowed artificial canyons.

The Outlander Club provides the setting for a variety of wildly differing purposes. Some of the gambling club's clientele come here looking for a good time, and nothing more, but just as many come looking for something else altogether. After all, in the endless metropolis of Coruscant, the discerning buyer can find almost anything, if they know where to look, and the Outlander Club is just the sort of place to look.

Mixing with the risk-taking glitterati are low-life slythmongers and con artists, looking for their next gullible victims.

The Outlander is far from the protection of Coruscant's regular security force. It is policed instead by self-proclaimed law enforcers, vigilantes who choose to defend the people on their turf from the criminals who would prey on the weak without their intervention.

As you walk up to the luridly-lit club, a pair of these enforcers – hard-faced Klatooinians, by the look of them – stop you at the door, hands hovering over the pocket blasters they have holstered at their belts.

"A Jedi," the taller of the two sneers. "Don't get many of your kind coming into the underlevels, bothering themselves with matters down here."

"No, that's usually left up to us," his wardman mutters, unimpressed.

"So, what brings you to the Outlander?" the first asks.

"I'm meeting someone," you tell the enforcer.

"There are a lot of people in tonight. So which one are you meeting up with? It's not Zorrian Platt, is it? I've heard he's hanging around again. But then I saw Goshan the Drak earlier, perhaps it's him. Ah, but a Jedi like you, maybe it's Koro Ferbin you're after."

Who will you say you have come to the Outlander Club to meet? Maybe it would be best to throw them off track?

If you say Zorrian Platt, turn to page 38.

If you say Goshan the Drak, click on box D on screen and type code DRAK or turn to page 105.

If you say Koro Ferbin, turn to page 65.

18 Jabba pronounces your punishment.

"You have been found guilty of coming to Jabba's palace to murder him,"TC-70 informs you, as you are cuffed. "You shall be taken to the Great Pit of Carkoon, there to be fed to the Sarlacc."

You are taken from the throne room and thrown into one of the many stinking cells in the dungeons below, while Jabba and his court transfer to the crime lord's massive luxury sail barge the *Khetanna*. When all is ready, you are unceremoniously taken on-board a smaller sand skiff and then the entire party sets out across the vast expanse of the Northern Dune Sea, crossing the Bantha Plains and B'omarr flats on its way to the Great Pit of Carkoon.

It does not take long for the *Khetanna* and its entourage to reach its morbid destination. Jabba's sail barge takes up a position over one side of the pit, affording Jabba and his guest of honour – the poisonous Asajj Ventress – a grandstand view of your execution, as the sand skiff bearing you and your Gamorrean guards glides to a halt directly over the pit. A gangplank extends from the side of the hovering skiff and you are forced out onto it.

Standing at the end of the gangplank you dare to look down into the Great Pit of Carkoon and see the writhing tentacles, inward-pointing teeth and thrusting beaked tongue of the monstrous Sarlacc. It is said that it takes the beast 1,000 years to digest its victims.

Jabba croaks one last utterance to you that is relayed via speakers booming from the sail barge. "The merciful Jabba wonders whether you have anything to say, any last words?" TC-70 asks.

This is the last chance you have to save yourself. You had better make it good.

"Only this, O wise and mighty Jabba," you say, as you stare down into the vast maw of the Sarlacc. "I ask that you give me one last chance to prove my innocence, by challenging my sworn enemy to single combat. At least let me go out fighting; it will make the spectacle of my death all the more entertaining, if you do."

For a moment an uneasy silence hangs over the pit, other than the whistling of the wind, as it blows swirling dust devils across the face of the desert before it. And then the Hutt's voice booms from the speakers on his sail barge again.

"Very well," TC-70 translates. "The most beneficent Jabba grants your request."

You watch Ventress's reaction from across the gulf of the void between you over the Great Pit of Carkoon. The shocked look on her face says it all.

Turn to page 184.

20 It does not take you long to reach the flight deck and when you get there you discover that it is just like the rest of the ship you have already passed through – utterly deserted.

Gazing out through the view shield you are horrified to see the mushroom-dome shape of the Senate hove into view ahead of the freighter. You have only a matter of seconds to stop the freighter from hitting its target, so you will need to choose your next move wisely. You don't have any time to waste.

If you want to take the helm immediately, turn to page 51.

If you want to check the freighter's autopilot before doing anything else, turn to page 92.

22 Bringing your craft around, you activate the starfighter's weapons system and choose your target. With the cargo bay doors in your sights, you open fire with both dual laser cannons. The doors disintegrate in an explosion of super-focused light energy.

Speed being of the essence, you bring the starfighter down – without even bothering to deploy its undercarriage first – pop the cockpit and leap out before the craft has even finished sliding to a halt.

As you whirl your Padawan's cloak about you, looking for signs directing you to the flight deck, an electronic whistle and chirrup of bleeps reminds you that you have not come here alone.

If you want to wait for R2-X4 to release itself and take the droid with you, turn to page 150.

If you do not want to delay at all, not knowing how long you might have before the freighter reaches its target, turn to page 20.

23 You accompany Commander Fox and his men as they carry out their shakedown of Coruscant's underlevels. Fox's investigations take you from the spires of the topmost levels of Galactic City to its seedier depths, hundreds of storeys beneath its artificial surface.

The last lead takes you to a haulier's hangar, which claims to be able to provide every kind of transport imaginable for the discerning customer. It was from here that the freighter used in the attack on the Senate was hired.

As the clone troopers take up positions around the rundown premises, Commander Fox signals two of his men to follow him into the hangar. You can't help wondering whether the commander's approach is a little heavy-handed and will get the results you're hoping for – the identity of the terrorist who set the freighter on its collision course with the Republic Senate.

If you want to go along with Commander Fox's plan and go after the clone troopers in force, turn to page 10.

If you want to suggest to the clone commander that you could try a more subtle approach, turn to 75.

24 You hurry through the maze-like halls of the building, heading for the Chancellor's private offices. It would be easy to get lost in the vast building, if it wasn't for the fact that you have accompanied your Master, Shaak Ti, to the Senate a number of times before.

The desperate tide of creatures passing you, heading in the opposite direction, is starting to thin now, as everyone evacuates the building. You spin around a corner, on the way to the express turbo-lift that will take you to the Chancellor's office, and run straight into a party of Wookiees from the lush forest world of Kashyyyk.

The Wookiees rise up before you, bellowing their fear and anger, and shaking their ceremonial war-staves at you, the plaited braids of their manes shaking in their fury. How will you respond to the Wookiees' bellowing challenge?

If you choose to draw your lightsaber and show them that you are armed, turn to page 48.

If you want to make a grovelling bow before them and then stand aside, turn to page 89.

25 With a jerk of the reins and kicking your heels into its heaving sides, you urge the large and lumbering dewback into the narrow valley pass between the rearing cliffs.

Your plan works. As soon as you are between the looming crags the lurking sniper opens fire. But you are ready for the attack and deflect the Tusken raider's shots with your lightsaber.

However, you are not ready for the other three snipers who are hidden on the opposite side of the gorge. A succession of bullets slams into your unprotected body from multiple rifle muzzles.

Seeing you fall to the Tusken Raiders' ambush saves Harlon Nayl's caravan, but it doesn't do much for your mission. Your adventure ends here.

THE END

26 "Get us out of here!" you shout to the pilot in the cockpit.

The gunship pulls up at the last possible minute, narrowly avoiding a head-on collision with the doomed starfighter. As the clone pilot takes your LAAT/i out of the immediate danger zone, all you can do is watch as the bounty hunter's ship finally comes down in the lake of liquid metal and quickly sinks below the surface, leaving no trace whatsoever that it was ever there at all.

With Vogg Barakk's death in the fiery lake of molten ore, the trail goes cold. Your only known route to finding out who was ultimately behind the attack on the Galactic Senate is dead. All you can do is make your way back to the Senate district, rendezvous with Master Shaak Ti and tell her of your failure . . . and watch the skies, waiting for the next attack to come. Your adventure is over.

THE END

27 You board the sand skiff the crime lord has sent to pick you up along with the protocol droid and set off across the parched ochre desert of Tatooine. The rippling sands of the Dune Sea sweep by underneath as the skiff eats up the kilometres between Mos Espa and Jabba's palace.

You pass the sun-bleached bones of long dead behemoths of the desert – the skeletons of banthas and greater krayt dragons – and at last come in sight of the crime lord's stronghold. As you gaze upon Jabba's citadel for the first time, you start to wonder what you are letting yourself in for by coming here.

The imposing fortress, that is now the lair of one of the most feared creatures in the galaxy, stands on the horizon amidst the rocky uplands that rise from the edge of the Northern Dune Sea.

The sand skiff sweeps round in front of the palace, turning off the cracked and pitted highway that leads to the main gate, and comes round behind the citadel. It enters through a hangar located at the rear, giving you a clear view of Jabba's impressive Ubrikkian sail barge as it glides past and finally comes to rest at the entrance to a broad, gloomy tunnel.

"Welcome to the official residence of his most beneficent Jabba the Hutt. Please follow me," the protocol droid says, turning and shuffling off into the tunnel beyond. Aware that a pair of Gamorrean guards has dropped into line behind you, effectively flanking you, you feel that you have little choice other than to do as you are told.

Turn to page 136.

28 Emerging from the Senate building behind the Chancellor and his honour guard, you risk a look at the sky, mindful of the ever-present danger the attack on the Senate poses. What you see there fills you with dread.

The Trandoshan freighter can be seen quite clearly now as it draws nearer. It is going to collide with the Senate at any moment. You are too late.

And then suddenly, incredibly, the vessel changes course, the snub nose of the ship rising sharply and you feel relief wash through you as it clears the Senate with a sonic boom. You watch as the freighter, now being accompanied by a flight of fire-suppression ships, heads off towards a safe landing site. The Senate is safe!

The immediate danger having passed, you turn your attention to where the Chancellor is now in close conversation with Shaak Ti, at the foot of the access ramp to the Chancellor's personal shuttle craft. You can guess what they are talking about and it makes you feel sick to the pit of your stomach.

Their conversation concluded, you wait at the edge of the landing pad as Master Ti approaches you, a disappointed expression on her face.

"The Chancellor tells me that you were responsible for a severe breach of protocol during the crisis and that you single-handedly nearly caused a diplomatic incident with the Wookiees," she says, in that still so calm voice of hers.

You feel that you would prefer it if she were shouting at you right now. You don't know what to say so you say nothing, staring uncomfortably at your feet instead.

"Diplomacy is an important part of a Jedi's role," she explains.

"I am sorry, Master. It won't happen again."

"That's right, it won't happen again. I have taken moves to make sure of it. The crisis here on Coruscant will not be over until we discover who was behind the attack on the Senate today. We need to find out who chartered that freighter and set it on a collision course."

Hope starts to swell within you once more; is Master Ti really going to give you another chance to prove yourself?

"You are to aid Commander Fox in his investigation of this matter."

You can't help but feel crestfallen. You were sure that Shaak Ti was going to give you the chance to redeem yourself, not have you babysat by a clone trooper.

If you want to challenge Master Ti's decision, turn to page 70.

If you simply want to accept her decision without making any fuss, turn to page 23.

30 You charge at Ventress, igniting your lightsaber as you go and bringing the glowing blue blade of your weapon up over your head.

As she brings her own crimson sabers to bear, you see the expression on Ventress's face go from one of shocked surprise, to horror, to cruel delight. Just as you are about to cut her down where she stands, you suddenly find yourself yanked off your feet and dangled above the ground by one leg.

With everything inverted before your eyes, your lightsaber slipping from your fingers and tumbling to the floor of the pit beneath you, you find yourself staring into the gaping maw of the hungry rancor. It is the last thing you ever see.

Your adventure ends here, as a tasty snack for Jabba's half-starved pet.
THE END

31 Shooting a glance downwards, at the cavernous void between the skyscraping buildings and the overlapping lanes of traffic, you choose your moment as best you can – considering the circumstances – and then, your heart in your mouth and taking a deep breath, you let go of the droid before it can do anything to harm you.

You drop for what seems like a long time, the cold wind of Coruscant's upper levels whipping at your face and cloak. And then you see the repulsor taxi rushing up to meet you.

The taxi lurches as you land on the back seat and a startled alien Aleena looks round to see who has just dropped in to join him.

"Follow that droid!" you command the driver, with a wave of your hand, before the alien can say anything.

"Follow that droid," he repeats, and, gunning the throttle, hurtles off after the assassin droid.

The droid eventually leads you to the Works district of the city-planet where it enters a crumbling carbonite refinery. You are certain that the villain you have been hunting has his hideout in there, but are you prepared to face the individual responsible for the attack on the Senate by yourself?

If you want to go in alone, turn to page 97.

If you want to contact Commander Fox and wait for the Coruscant Guard to arrive before doing anything else, turn to page 146.

33 Jabba takes a moment to consider your proposal and then mutters something in Huttese in his deep booming voice.

"The most magnificent Lord Jabba agrees to your request," TC-70 says, without any hint of emotion. "You shall face your accuser Asajj Ventress in mortal combat."

"What? Surely you jest, noble Jabba," Ventress exclaims. She starts to back away, her twin lightsabers leaping into her hands in an instant.

But Jabba has not finished making his proclamation yet. "And the most esteemed Jabba decrees that the duel shall take place within the rancor pit," TC-70 finishes.

The rancor pit? Both you and Ventress look down at your feet, realizing that you are both standing on a large metal grille set into the floor. At the same moment the vast trapdoor swings open beneath you, dropping both of you – Jedi and Dark Acolyte – into the stinking pit below.

You and Ventress get to your feet, eyeing one another suspiciously and igniting your lightsabers, watchful as to who might try to make the first move.

The groaning of ropes and the creaking of ancient pulleys draws your attention to the gate that is now rising on the other side of the cave-pit. A huge claw slips through the widening gap and grasps the bottom of the gate, helping to push it up into the groove in the rock above. With an enraged roar, the rancor enters the pit.

The monster stands five metres tall and is just as broad, with a flat blunt head, large fanged maw dripping with digestive spittle, and long grasping claws. Snorting with furious animal aggression it starts to lumber towards you.

"Jedi!" Ventress calls to you across the pit. "Listen to me if you want to live!"

All the while the monster is closing the distance between it and its next meal – you!

If you want to listen to what Asajj Ventress has to say, click box L on screen and type code word VENTRESS or turn to page 179.

If you would rather ignore her and prepare to battle the charging rancor, turn to page 44.

35 Mos Espa is one of Tatooine's largest spaceports but it is also a rough, lawless town inhabited by poor settlers and controlled by powerful gangsters. Those who call the sand-blasted domes home eke out an existence through scavenging, trading, gambling and even stealing.

Trying your best to keep a low profile on this backwater world, in case your identity as a Jedi attracts the interest of spies working for either Jabba the Hutt or Count Dooku's Separatists, you decide how best to traverse the many kilometres of barren wilderness that lie between the rundown spaceport of Mos Espa and Jabba's Palace over sixty kilometres away.

After spending some time exploring the markets and vehicle rental shops on the outskirts of the spaceport, you narrow it down to two options. You could either find employ with a spice merchant as his bodyguard and travel with his caravan as it heads south-east over the Great Mesa Plateau, or you could use the galactic credits the Temple furnished you with before your departure from Coruscant to buy yourself a beat up old landspeeder.

If you want to join the spice merchant as a bodyguard, turn to page 80.

If you want to purchase a landspeeder to cross the open desert more quickly, but alone, turn to page 52.

36 The stranger sidles up to you when you are queuing at one of the many food outlets located on-board the ship to cater for the thousands of refugees that make up the majority of its cargo.

"Hey," he whispers in your ear, "you're that Jedi, aren't you?"

How could he possibly know that? You're in disguise, the hood of your cloak hiding your Padawan braid. And who is he anyway?

"Who are you?" you hiss, keeping your voice down so as not to draw attention to yourself.

"I'm . . . a friend," the alien says. "You're not safe here. There's a-, an assassin on-board, looking for you. If you want to live, come with me."

He moves out of the queue for food, beckoning for you to follow him.

If you want to go with the stranger, turn to page 82.

If you want to stay where you are, turn to page 121.

37 Focusing your mind and reaching out with the splayed fingers of one hand, you use the power of the Force to slow and then finally stop Padmé's fall altogether. Sweat beading on your brow from the effort, you manage to raise the Senator up to the side of the speeder through sheer force of willpower, until Shaak Ti can pull her back on-board. The Senator is safe. Unfortunately the same cannot be said for you.

Suddenly Ventress is there in the skiff with you, having vaulted back across the divide on to the hovering sand skiff. She swiftly cuts down Jabba's guards whilst deftly deflecting the shots of the clone troopers accompanying Shaak Ti. Drained by your manipulation of the Force, you stumble towards Ventress as she seizes control of the skiff and prepares to use it to make her escape.

You stagger up behind her but, just when you thought you still had the element of surprise, she spins round and plants a vicious kick in your sternum. The blow sends you reeling backwards, into the gunwale of the skiff, and you topple over into the pit.

As Asajj Ventress makes her escape, the Sarlacc sets to work digesting you. You may have helped stop the Separatist's treacherous plans but in the end you could not save yourself. Your adventure and your life are over.

THE END

38 "Is that so?" the enforcer says with a cold look in his feral eyes. "Then you'd better come with us."

You follow the Klatooinians as they lead you through the noisy club – with its bright lights and pounding offworld beats – leaving the bar and the packed dancefloor behind until you they stop beside the wall between two stalls.

The lead enforcer beats on the wall panel with his fist and a moment later it swings open. The enforcers lead you through the secret door and along the darkened passageway revealed beyond.

You eventually emerge in an old warehouse, buried deep within the Coruscant underlevels, and come face-to-face with a figure whose face is hidden by the black robes that cover his body. It is only then that your Jedi senses start to tell you that something might be wrong.

"I hear you're looking for the bounty hunter Zorrian Platt," the mysterious stranger says, in an electronically distorted voice.

"Th-That's right," you reply uncertainly, reaching for where your lightsaber is hanging from your belt.

"Well, you've found him," the bounty hunter says, whipping a blaster from the holster at his waist. "But I don't know you and I don't need any do-gooder Jedi getting in my way."

You barely have time to thumb the activation stud on your lightsaber before Zorrian Platt shoots you at point blank range. Your adventure is over.

THE END

39 The two remaining gunships soar through the gigantic dust clouds thrown up by the toppling towers of the factory as the ancient structure finally collapses behind you, after countless centuries of neglect.

And then you see Vogg Barakk's starfighter above you, silhouetted against the fiery sky. But the clone gunships' attack on the Works has flushed out more than just the bounty hunter you are chasing. As the LAAT/is bear down on the starfighter, another vessel – this time a heavily-modified Corellian freighter – blasts clear of the demolition zone.

"That's the *Nebray Manta*, Kozzel Qwok's ship," Commander Fox informs you. "We've been hunting that Pacithhip smuggler for months. It could just be possible that he had something to do with the attack on the Senate. We've long suspected a link between Qwok's gang and Count Dooku's Separatists, and now he's running too."

"So who do we go after?" you ask.

"What do your instincts tell you?" Commander Fox replies.

Who do you think you should pursue?

If you want to keep after Vogg Barakk, turn to page 107.

If you want to change tack and go after the Pacithhip smugglers instead, turn to page 13.

40 Igniting your lightsaber and with a furious shout, you leap through the archway and into the throne room, somersaulting through the air to land between the would-be assassin and Jabba the Hutt.

"A Jedi," Asajj Ventress hisses, igniting the crimson sabers that are already in her hands.

She meets your initial lunge and, although you valiantly defend yourself against the hairless, grey-skinned dark sider, you are no match for her. Ventress has fought both Obi-Wan Kenobi and Anakin Skywalker, and lived to tell the tale.

She comes at you like an enraged wampa, locking her twin blades together to form a deadly saberstaff. You really don't stand a chance. Your adventure ends here, as you are cut down by the Dark Acolyte's whirling blades before the excited gaze of Jabba the Hutt.

THE END

41 "Master Ti," you say, your eyes straying to the docking platform behind you. "I believe there may be another way, to save not only Chancellor Palpatine but also the Senate building itself."

"What is it you are suggesting, Padawan?" the Togruta asks, following your gaze towards the various spaceships squatting there on the landing pad, looking like gleaming metal insects.

"If I took a craft and rendezvoused with the freighter, I could steer it away from the Senate altogether."

Shaak Ti regards you with an inscrutable stare. "Very well," she says at last. "Do it. Commander Fox, the Chancellor's safety is your responsibility now."

"Yes, General!"

As the troopers of the Coruscant Guard set about evacuating the Senate, you run for the docking platform.

Two suitable craft stand side by side on the landing pad; a gleaming yellow Jedi starfighter and a battered green airspeeder that looks like it has seen better days.

If you want to take the green airspeeder, turn to page 113.

If you want to intercept the freighter using the Jedi starfighter, click on box A on screen and type code word YELLOW or turn to page 68.

42 The second LAAT/i cannot resist the barrage of laser and missile fire that suddenly comes its way. You can do nothing to help the clone troopers on-board as their craft plummets into the burning lake of molten ore that lies at the heart of an automated manufactory. All you can do is ensure that their sacrifice has not been in vain, by bringing the bounty hunter to justice. Vogg Barakk will not escape you this time.

Following the trajectory of its swooping dive, the bounty hunter's vessel comes in low over the lake just as a plume of fire is thrown high into the scorching air as a hidden gas bubble bursts. The eruption catches the starfighter's wing, dousing it with great gobbets of molten metal.

Even now, it seems that Vogg Barakk may yet escape justice, as suddenly the tables are turned on the Snivvian bounty hunter. His ship starts to lose height rapidly, as its port engine fails. The only way to save him now, so that the Jedi might still interrogate him, is to risk your own life.

If you want to attempt to rescue Vogg Barakk from otherwise certain death, click box G on screen and type code word RESCUE or turn to page 72.

If you want to leave the bounty hunter to his fate, and get out of here as quickly as you can before your gunship shares the fate of the starfighter, turn to page 26.

44 You're not going to listen to a word Ventress has to say. To do so would be to take the first step on the path to the dark side and that is something you could never do.

The time for words has passed. Action is what is needed now if you are to win your duel with Ventress and escape the clutches of the half-starved rancor. But which one of them do you want to take on first?

If you want to go after Ventress before she can engineer her escape, turn to page 30.

If you would rather deal with Jabba's gruesome pet first, turn to page 102.

45 You come to, lying amidst the detritus of a water-logged rubbish swamp, with the rubbery tendril of a conduit worm probing your ear, as the creature looks for a suitable place to burrow. Batting the worm away, you sit up and take in your surroundings.

Your fall was cushioned by a matt of knotted weeds, that have grown to claim what might once have been either a mound of discarded rubbish or perhaps even the wreckage of a downed speeder, for all you know.

Wiping a film of oily black water from your face you peer into the near-permanent gloom of this strange underworld in which you have landed. A strange glow pervades this realm, given off by a variety of phosphorescent moss and a swirling bioluminescence in the water that glows a bright blue every time something disturbs the surface of the swamp.

If you didn't know any better, you could almost believe that you weren't on Coruscant at all. The fetid swamp spreads out in all directions, as far as your eyes can see through the murky gloom. Strange clicks and croaks echo across the marshy hollows and strange pallid plants – some of which you're sure are moving – cling to the pillared footings of the skyscrapers that soar above you, leaving this mist-cloaked mire in a state of permanent darkness.

You need to get out of this place and fast. You dread to think what might be lurking down here with you and the longer you delay, the more likely the villain behind the attack on the Senate is to make his escape, probably offworld somewhere. You decide to contact Commander Fox before doing anything else, only to discover that your comlink is fouled with swamp water and no longer working.

A large lump breaks the surface of a pool nearby and then submerges again. A moment later you feel the pontoon on which you are resting lurch as something slides underneath. If you are going to get out of this place at all you are going to have to do so alone.

Enough rubbish has been captured by the swamp to create a series of stepping stones, paths and islands by which you should be able to negotiate this treacherous domain but which way will you go?

With no way of scaling the sheer, slime-slicked walls of the canyon you are going to have to follow it in one direction or the other. In one direction – east, you think – the swamp continues for as far as you can see. The other way, the swamp ends at the entrance to a network of tunnels formed by the arching supports of skyscrapers.

If you want to set out across the swamp, click box F on screen and type code word SWAMP, or turn to page 160.

If you want to head for the tunnels, turn to page 98.

47 There is no way you are willingly going to lay down your weapon when you are surrounded by Gamorrean Guards, out-of-work mercenaries and some of the galaxy's most ruthless bounty hunters, not to mention the enemy of the Jedi, Asajj Ventress herself.

"I beg your forgiveness, noble Jabba, but the Rattatakan cannot be trusted," you say, "and so, although it pains me greatly, I cannot submit to your wishes."

The bloated slug barks another command and four of his Gamorrean bodyguards push their way from the crowd of onlookers to surround you.

"Mighty Jabba is most displeased," the protocol droid tells you, in a disappointed tone as the guards seize you.

Turn to page 18.

48 Taking your lightsaber from your belt, you thumb the activation switch and a blade of crystal blue light hums into existence from the haft of the weapon. You bring the energy blade up before your face in a two-handed grip, ready to defend yourself against the angry Wookiees.

The Wookiees take a step backwards, suddenly cowed. A feral snarl escapes their leader's curled lips. You do not need to be able to speak Shyriiwook to know that you have made no friends here. The evac alarm continues to echo through the empty corridors. The situation is so tense you could cut the atmosphere with your lightsaber.

"What is the meaning of this?" a voice as sharp and clear as crystal asks.

The Wookiee party immediately withdraws and the imperious figure of Chancellor Palpatine steps between them, coming to a halt in front of you. To either side of the man stand his two most trusted confidantes – Speaker of the Senate, Mas Amedda, and his staff aide, Sly Moore. The Wookiees bow their heads reverentially in the presence of the Chancellor.

You feel your face flush red and your heart race, suddenly finding yourself in the presence of Palpatine and in such an embarrassing situation. You immediately deactivate your lightsaber and bow your head in shame.

He fixes you with a piercing gaze. "Explain yourself, young Jedi," he says with authority.

"M-My apologies, Chancellor," you begin, "but I was sent by Master Shaak Ti of the Jedi Temple to ensure your safety. The Senate is under attack. We must evacuate immediately."

Palpatine's expression remains grave. "Which is precisely what we were doing." He turns to the Wookiee delegates. "My apologies, Senator Yarua," he says with the utmost decorum, "but let us not delay any longer. It would appear that we are all in peril. But have no fear," he says, throwing you a dark look, "I assure you that I shall personally see to it that this Padawan's insolence does not go unpunished."

With that, Palpatine and his entourage sweep past you, making for the landing platform where a shuttle is waiting to carry the Chancellor to safety. The Wookiees follow close on the heels of the Chancellor's party while you trail along behind, lost in a world of shame and embarrassment.

Turn to page 28.

50 Reaching the end of the corridor, you turn into the passageway beyond and almost collide with a pair of pug-faced Gamorrean Guards. The dull-witted Gamorreans grunt in surprise and then make a grab for you.

Caught off guard and against two brawny examples of an alien species known for its great strength and resilience, it isn't long before you find yourself their prisoner. The Gamorreans drag you off, between them, deeper into the dungeons of the palace to meet with whatever fate it is they have in mind for you.

Turn to page 151.

51 You throw yourself into the pilot's position and, seizing hold of the freighter's con-stick, pull back to lift the freighter clear of the Senate . . . but nothing happens!

No matter how much you work the controls, the freighter remains locked on its collision course with the Galactic Senate.

The navicom must be locked. You will need to disengage the autopilot before you can do anything to change the direction in which the freighter's heading.

Turn to page 92.

52 The landspeeder is a beat-up old X-34 class but it will serve its purpose – even though you have the feeling that the vendor saw an opportunity to make a few extra credits when you walked through his door. But at least it's better – and quicker – than slogging across the Northern Dune Sea on foot.

You have been travelling for some hours already, when you come to the canyons that border the Great Mesa Plateau. To trace a path between the towering peaks would be the most direct way to reach Jabba's Palace and so you guide the landspeeder into the network of canyons, crevasses and chasms.

You have not gone far when you hear the echoing roars of what sounds like some huge animal, as they travel back to you from the twisting canyon ahead of you.

You have heard that Tatooine is home to a number of large predators, including the massiff and the howler. Could one of them be waiting for you at the end of this pass?

If you want to continue heading into the canyon, click box H on screen and type code word CANYON, or turn to page 71.

If you want to quit the canyons and head out over the Northern Dune Sea to find a safer – as well as longer – route to Jabba's Palace, turn to page 126.

53 Re-tracing your steps back around the last corner you passed, you duck behind a founder's statue that is standing inside an alcove in the wall.

You wait, your heart pounding against your ribs, trying to stop your breath coming in harsh gasps. A moment later, the Blue Guard who stopped you at the door to the Senate Chamber trots past, trying to make it to safety himself now. You only wait long enough for him to round the next corner before emerging from your hiding place again.

The corridor is completely deserted now. You begin to think that there really isn't anyone left in the building, but you still cannot leave until you have done all you can to be certain that Chancellor Palpatine is safe.

You fling open the door to the Senate Chamber and find yourself standing at the edge of a vast amphitheatre. The circular bowl of the Great Rotunda is lined with the 1,024 platforms used by the sectorial Senators and others who would address the Senate themselves. But there is no one here now – every single one of them is empty – and the Chancellor's own podium has been retracted beneath the iris-opening floor of the chamber.

So if Chancellor Palpatine isn't here, where is he?

If you want to go to the Chancellor's holding office located directly beneath the Great Rotunda to look for him, turn to page 14.

If you want to make your way to Palpatine's private offices, elsewhere within the massive Senate building, turn to page 106.

54 You catch up with the bounty hunter's vessel again over a metal smelting plant, only to discover that the starfighter is in trouble. Black smoke is streaming from the starboard engine. It is obvious that the ship is going down, and it is heading straight for the bubbling lake of molten metal that lies at the heart of the automated processing plant.

Your LAAT/i chases after the plummeting Corellian freighter but you are too late to save the Snivvian. There is nothing you can do but watch, as the bounty hunter's craft hits the seething lake of liquid metal and quickly sinks below its surface, leaving no trace whatsoever that it was ever there.

With Vogg Barakk's death in the fiery lake of molten ore, the trail goes cold. Your only route to finding out who was ultimately behind the attack on the Galactic Senate is dead. The only thing you can do is make your way back to the Senate district, rendezvous with Master Shaak Ti and tell her of your failure . . . and watch the skies, waiting for the next attack to come. Your mission is over.

THE END

55 You decide that you don't have time to waste waiting to speak to a short-order chef who may, or may not, have heard something about someone planning something . . .

It's time you tried another approach, but the only one left open to you is to join Commander Fox in his underworld shakedown.

Calling the clone commander on your comlink, you board an air taxi and make for city bottom, ready to rendezvous with the Coruscant Guard.

Turn to page 23.

56 You chase after the assassin droid as it buzzes away from the city bottom haulier's, returning to whoever programmed it to hunt down the Toydarian, now that its murderous mission is complete.

You chase the buzzing droid through the artificial canyons of the underlevels but you can't keep up the pace for much longer and realize that if you don't do something fast, the droid is going to get away from you.

In a moment of recklessness you throw yourself at the droid, as it starts to levitate out of reach, using your Jedi powers to launch yourself even higher. For a moment it looks like the assassin droid might yet get away from you, but then your hands close around the fins of the droid's flight stabilizing wings and you hang on for dear life.

The droid's flight path dips for a moment and then starts to climb again rapidly as it leaves Coruscant's underlevels far behind, carrying you closer and closer towards the multi-layered lanes of air traffic hurtling between the mountainous skyscrapers of the world-city. You must be thousands of feet up by now!

Your arrival in the traffic lanes is met by the vibrant glow of bright neon lights, the blur of speeding vehicles and the blaring of air-horns. As if it wasn't bad enough that everything from airbuses to *Firespray*-class patrol ships are now trying to avoid hitting you, the outer casing of the droid starts to crackle with electricity.

Is something wrong with the droid or is it preparing to use some sort of anti-personnel measure against you?

If you want to keep a tight hold of the assassin droid, turn to page 118.

If you would rather let go now and deal with the consequences, turn to page 31.

58 As you bring the freighter level again, you desperately search for a suitable landing site amidst the columns and spires of the Senatorial district, but can see none.

Then, at the last possible moment it seems, you spot an emergency landing strip lying between a City Municipal Authorities building and a skyscraping hotel.

The freighter's failing engines mean that you have to land before you can even deploy the landing gear. The impact of your forced crash-landing nearly throws you out of the pilot's seat and through the view-shield.

The freighter travels another half a kilometre before finally juddering to a halt amidst a flight of fussing emergency vehicles, which douse the ship's engines with jets of flame-retardant foam before they overload and explode.

But as your flight trainer used to say, a good landing is one you can walk away from, and minutes later you stagger clear of the crumpled hull of the freighter and across the scorched runway to a chorus of cheers and rapturous applause from the assembled ground crews.

You have saved the Senate, and prevented the freighter's crash-landing from causing any loss of life – including your own! You are a hero!

Turn to page 11.

59 The crime lord barks something in Huttese and his protocol droid TC-70 patiently translates for your benefit.

"The honourable Jabba does not agree to your request. You came here by stealth and subterfuge and Jabba is wise to your wiles. You are not to be trusted."

At that, Ventress begins to laugh cruelly, mocking you and your dire predicament.

Turn to page 123.

60 As night spreads its veil of darkness over the ochre sands of the Northern Dune Sea, you scamper past the huge scrap pile constructed from all the metal waste thrown out from the palace, without being spotted. Having waited for a jabbering pair of Jawas – dragging a battered R4 unit after them – to pass by, when the coast is clear you duck inside the ominous black opening of the tunnel mouth.

You have to stoop to proceed any distance along the tunnel – the Jawas who dug it out of the hillside being considerably shorter than the average human – using the flickering blue glow of your activated lightsaber to light your way.

After creeping about in near-darkness, bent almost double for nearly an hour, as you follow the twists and turns of the passageway, you finally see a light at the end of the tunnel.

You ease open a grilled vent and clamber through it into a gloomy subterranean corridor formed from a series of stone-cut archways. A musty atmosphere permeates the place and you can hear the murmur of what sounds like burbling cantina music echoing along the corridor from somewhere else deep within the citadel.

Hearing a gruff grunting sound you duck into cover behind a pillar as a pair of Jabba's brutish, green-skinned Gamorrean guards round the bend of the passageway ahead of you, grim-looking vibro-lances in hand. You were only just in time but fortunately they didn't see you and so trudge straight past your hiding place.

Just when you think it's safe to move on, you hear a sharp chattering behind you and you look back up the tunnel to see a pair of hooded Jawa faces peering out of the still open vent-grille. Their shrill jabbering voices alert the dull-witted Gamorreans who turn around in time to see you trying to make your getaway.

But even as you prepare to defend yourself with your glowing lightsaber, another pair of pug-faced Gamorreans appears from the other end of the dusty passageway and you find yourself surrounded.

You are about to engage the first of the ugly creatures in single combat when you remember your mission. You have come here to find out whether Jabba the Hutt really was behind the attack on the Senate on Coruscant, and face to face might be the best way. So it is that you deactivate your lightsaber and put up your hands in surrender, ready for the Gamorrean guards to take you into custody.

Turn to page 151.

62 Deciding that you have nothing to lose, you pay the Trandoshan from the credits given to you by the Temple to help you complete your mission, and then hope that he has information that will be of use.

You start by telling Gha Nachkt about the attack on the Senate and the attempt on Chancellor Palpatine's life. "I heard about that," he says. "There was an Iktotchi in here talking about it earlier."

He continues to scratch at his chin with his long fingernails and, after some thought, says, "I don't know anything about any dodgy freighter-charters. Why would I? I am a purveyor of previously owned collector's items, not some criminal, but I know a man who might. Go to the Outlander Club and ask for Koro Ferbin."

Glad to have your dealings with the Trandoshan concluded, you leave the diner without even finishing your drink.

Turn to page 16.

63 You watch intently as the hairless assassin places her twin sabers on the ground in front of Jabba's dais and then bows low before the alien gangster.

"O mighty and generous Jabba Desilijic Tiure, I pledge my allegiance to you," Ventress declares, in that sneering voice of hers. "I am yours. Direct me as you see fit."

What is going on here? Asajj Ventress, an agent of the dark side of the Force swearing allegiance to the Hutt Desilijic clan? It hardly seems credible. The treacherous assassin is obviously up to something and is not to be trusted.

This has gone on long enough; it is time you did something to stop her.

Igniting your lightsaber, with a shout of rage you leap into the throne room, somersaulting through the air to land between the Dark Acolyte and Jabba the Hutt.

The corpulent crime lord shouts something to his guards and although you cannot understand what he is saying, you understand its meaning plainly enough.

You are immediately surrounded by Jabba's elite Gamorrean guards. For a moment you consider putting up a fight but then realize that you are fiercely outnumbered. Such a move would result in at least one death, and that would be yours. You lower your lightsaber, flicking off the beam of its energy blade, and await the outcome of your actions.

"A Jedi," Asajj Ventress scowls, activating her own crimson sabers that are now back in her hands. "And so the assassin is revealed," she hisses, a cruel smile playing about her lips.

Turn to page 123.

65 Without saying another word, the enforcers step out of the way and admit you to the club. The Outlander attracts a mainly humanoid clientele and many of its patrons hide their identities behind elaborate masks. Even dressed in your traditional Jedi tunic and cloak, and with your uncut Padawan braid, you do not particularly stand out amongst those visiting the club tonight.

But now that you are inside you realize that you have no idea what Koro Ferbin looks like. How are you ever going to find him? And then Koro Ferbin finds you . . .

"Master Jedi," a voice calls from a table close by, "what brings you to such a disreputable den of reprobates as this?"

"The search for information," you reply.

"Information, you say? Then you've come to the right place," says the flamboyantly-dressed alien. "For I am an information broker; whatever you need, whether facts and figures, data or disinformation, you've come to the right place. Let me introduce myself." He stands, with a flourish of his colourful coat, and offers you his hand. "Koro Ferbin, at your service!"

With great relief you tell Koro all you know about the attack on the Senate.

"So what do you want to know?" Ferbin asks.

"I need to know who chartered that freighter," you tell him.

"Well, you know what they say." Ferbin looks at you furtively. "If the price is right . . ."

Before embarking on your mission, Shaak Ti provided you with
enough credits for just such a situation. Koro Ferbin's eyes light up as
he sees what you're offering and then happily divulges what you need
to know, providing you with a name, Vogg Barakk, and a location – the
Works!

Turn to page 186.

67 Not wanting to lose sight of the Techno Union starfighter for a second now that you've caught up with the bounty hunter at last, Commander Fox leads the gunship squadron between the skeletal hulks of the decayed factory complexes after the escaping Snivvian.

As the gunships close on the starfighter and come within effective firing range, the clones prepare to bring the craft down in a controlled manner. The bounty hunter obviously realizes that he is in danger of being caught and springs his trap. The dual laser cannons fixed to his starfighter's wings open fire, a stream of laser pulses tearing into the half-toppled structures between which you are passing.

The weakened factory buildings looming above you start to collapse straight away. It is crucial now, not that you catch up with the bounty hunter, but that all the Republic gunships get out in one piece.

As the LAAT/is split up – every pilot taking violent, evasive action; powering the craft forwards, up and out of the danger zone – a trailing LAAT/i fails to get clear before the toppling towers come crashing down with a deafening scream of shearing metal and the thunderous boom of crumbling structures.

And so it is that only two gunships climb clear the decaying dead zone, still in pursuit of the bounty hunter's ship.

Turn to page 39.

68 It takes you only a few seconds to settle yourself in the cockpit of the starfighter. You quickly power up the engine and an electronic chirrup tells you that the on-board astromech unit – designation R2-X4 – is ready to plot a course.

With the hum of rising power, the starfighter lifts off from the docking platform and gunning the engines you hurtle forwards at breakneck speed, ready to intercept the freighter.

The dirty black shape of the Trandoshan freighter soon swells to fill the visible view through the cockpit canopy.

Somehow you need to dock with the vessel while it is still some distance from the Senate, but you can see no easy way of doing so. However, you could always use the starfighter's laser cannons to blast a way in. Then again, you could try using the lasers to bring the freighter down before it ever reaches the Senate district.

If you want to use the starfighter's lasers to blast the cargo bay open, turn to page 22.

If you want to use the lasers to try to bring the ship down, turn to page 96.

69 You try to trick Ventress by feinting sideways, but balanced precariously as you are, it is you who loses your footing, and you drop off the end of the gangplank. You make a desperate lunge for the plank and grab hold of it with the fingertips of your free hand, abruptly arresting your potentially fatal fall.

As Ventress stalks towards you along the gangplank you feel it vibrate with every step she takes, and your fingertips start to slip.

If you want to let go of your lightsaber so that you can grab hold of the plank with both hands, turn to page 116.

If losing your lightsaber is the last thing you want to do, turn to page 177.

70 "Please, Master, I acted rashly only because I was so anxious to rescue Chancellor Palpatine, a task you entrusted to me yourself." You fall to your knees before the Jedi Master.

The Togruta regards you through narrowed eyes but says nothing.

"Please, I beg of you, give me one more chance to prove myself a worthy student of the Force. Let me undertake this mission alone."

"You were given the opportunity to prove yourself and almost caused a diplomatic incident. You have had your chance." Shaak Ti regards you closely. "You obviously need time to meditate on your failings. Return to the Temple while I consider whether I was too hasty to permit your elevation to Padawan. Wait for me there."

Return to the Temple? Things are going from bad to worse. You sense that you have one last chance to convince Master Ti that you can be trusted with this mission. If you don't say something now, you may never get the chance to put right the wrong you have done. But what could possibly convince the Jedi to change her mind?

If you want to be humble in your approach, turn to page 164.

If you want to show how capable you are by standing up to Shaak Ti, turn to page 122.

71 As Tatooine's twin suns set beyond the barrier of the chasm walls, you continue on your current course, following the canyon as it twists and turns left and right, around bend after bend, the snorting and bellowing sounds getting louder all the time.

And then you emerge into a broad gorge within this fractured landscape and find yourself in the shadow of a colossal behemoth of the desert that blocks the way onwards, its thick iron-hide the colour of rust. But this is no monster; it is an ancient sandcrawler, one of the mighty machines in the possession of the diminutive Jawas that negotiate the endless tracts of desert wilderness in search of salvage scrap, of which there is plenty.

Turn to page 104.

72 "We have to save Barakk," you tell Commander Fox, "otherwise the lives of the men you've lost today will have all been for nothing."

"Understood," Fox says, "but I hope you know what you're doing."

"I'll think of something," you reply, as the gunship banks sharply to come around alongside the starfighter as it drops towards the molten lake of fire.

And then a solution presents itself to you. Securing a line to the inside of the gunship's cabin, with your heart in your mouth and your lightsaber in your hand, you let out the line, dropping from the gunship over the wing of the starfighter, as the pilot skilfully matches its fatal trajectory with the LAAT/i.

You can see the bubbling orange lake of liquid metal below you, its seething surface getting closer all the time, the heat forcing your eyes closed when you look down and scalding your lungs as you breathe. But there is no time to think about that now.

Two sweeping arcs of your lightsaber break open the seals on the cockpit and you are able to pull the canopy free to reach the bounty hunter inside. Vogg Barakk looks up at you in startled surprise, the conflicting emotions of fear and relief warring for control of his pug-nosed features. Before he has time to decide to resist, you grab hold of the Snivvian and activate the reverse control on your line so that it starts to reel you and your prisoner back towards the gunship.

As soon as you are on-board along with your captive, the LAAT/i's pilot brings the gunship out of its fatal dive and clear of the lava lake. Vogg Barakk's starfighter crashes into the seething sea of molten ore, throwing up a great wave of liquid metal before it, and quickly disappears from view altogether.

Turn to page 124.

74 Choosing to travel to Tatooine by Jedi starfighter, you dock the one-man vessel with one of several hyperspace booster rings waiting in orbit over Coruscant and instruct your R2 unit to plot a course for Tatooine . . .

Dropping out of hyperspace at the edge of the Tatooine system, you detach your craft from the booster and take the starfighter in towards the dusty yellow ball that hangs suspended in the void of space, far from its famed twin suns.

Signalling the planet below, you make contact with the communications hub at Jabba the Hutt's palace and request an audience with the most merciful Jabba himself. Your request accepted, you take the starfighter down to the planet, before coming in to land not far from the B'omarr monastery that is now the notorious gangster's fortress.

It is with no small amount of trepidation that you approach the palace on foot, as Tatooine's twin suns set and a chill wind sweeps in from across the Northern Dune Sea.

Turn to page 144.

75 "Commander," you whisper into Fox's ear. "Surely there must be something else we can try, before you charge in all guns blazing."

The clone trooper turns to regard you and even though you can't see his features behind the darkened visor of his helmet you still feel his penetrating stare boring into you. You start to worry that you have overstepped the mark and offended the clone commander with your comments.

"What are you suggesting, Padawan?" the clone commander asks gruffly.

"Let me go in first, see if I can find out what we need to know using my Jedi influence," you say. "And if my plan doesn't work, we can resort to your strategy."

"Very well, let's see what you can do. Impress me."

With the weight of the clone commander's expectations upon you, you step out from behind the pile of crates and cautiously approach the haulier's hangar.

You push open the door and step into a clutter of repulsorlift parts that smell of lubricating oil and sweetspice. As the door closes behind you a bell jangles somewhere else on the premises.

"Whaddya want, hmm?" asks the trunk-nosed, blue-skinned Toydarian that appears from behind a heat exchanger unit, hovering above the ground on rapidly beating wings.

If you want to try to use a Jedi mind trick on the Toydarian to

wheedle the information you need out of him, turn to page 139.

If you want to try to persuade the Toydarian to help you without resorting to subterfuge, click box E on screen and type code word BHUTO or turn to page 114.

77 Although they continue to snort and grunt at you, thick strings of saliva slobbering over their blunt yellow tusks and shaking their weapons at you in a threatening manner, they do not actually attack.

A moment later, the protocol droid that they were supposed to be accompanying catches up with the Gamorreans and bustles past them imperiously.

"I do beg your pardon," the droid says extremely politely. "I do apologize for the welcome you have received from my colleagues but I am here now. I am protocol droid TC-70 and I welcome you on behalf of the most beneficent and bounteous Jabba the Hutt of the Desilijic clan. Please, follow me."

One of the Gamorreans also beckons you forward with a jerk of its snouted head and, not wanting to upset the guard, just in case, you set off after TC-70.

Turn to page 136.

78 You soon leave the trooper behind you as you press on into the labyrinthine halls of the Senate. But where will you begin your search for Chancellor Palpatine?

If you want to make for his suite of private offices, turn to page 24.

If you decide to head for the Senate meeting chamber itself, turn to page 134.

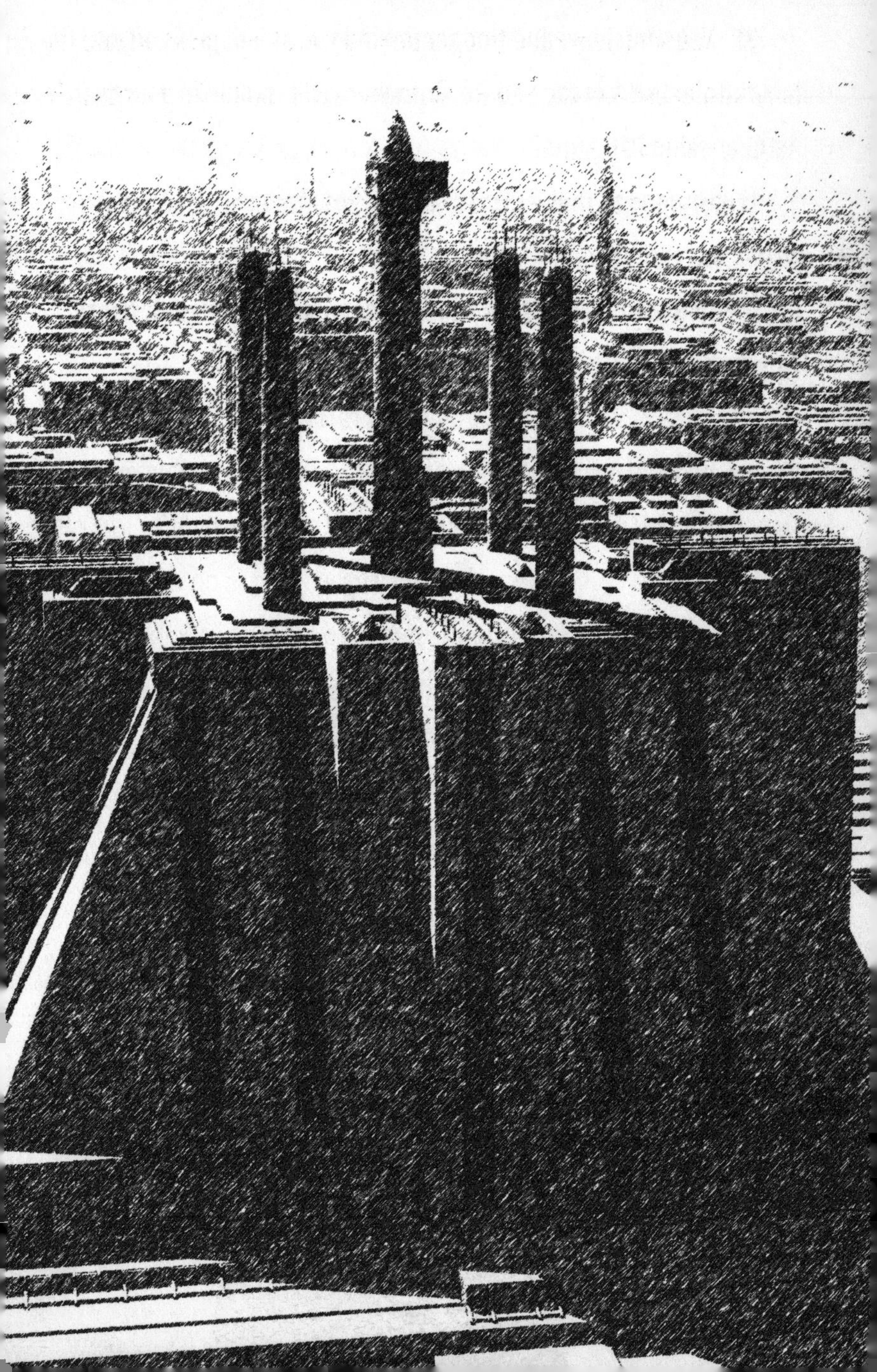

80 Once the merchant, one Harlon Nayl, has tied up his affairs in Mos Espa, the caravan sets off, with you in the saddle of a large, leathery-skinned dewback. Native to Tatooine, dewbacks make ideal beasts of burden as they are well-adapted to the harsh desert climate and can be easily domesticated.

The caravan follows an old slave traders' route through Beggar's Canyon and into the barren uplands of the Great Mesa Plateau. The cavalcade of wagons and repulsorlift carts are passing along a dried up river-bed when you spot the glint of sunlight on glass that gives away the hiding place of a sniper high in the hills to your left.

Borrowing a pair of electrobinoculars you zoom in on the cliff ledge and see the instantly recognizable, shrouded face of a Tusken raider. These natives of Tatooine are an aggressive species and violent enemies of the planet's moisture farmers, with whom they compete for precious water sources. They prey on the weak and will happily take pot-shots with their simple charged-projectile rifles at anyone who strays into their tribal lands.

You are sure that a Tusken ambush is awaiting the caravan ahead but to turn the whole lot around to find a different route through the desert would take a long time and might not prove to be any safer. It would also slow your own progress to Jabba the Hutt's palace significantly. You realize that you are going to have to simply deal with the Sand People yourself.

If you want to lead the caravan into the hills and then deal with the consequences of your actions, turn to page 25.

If you would rather climb into the crags, sneak up on the Sand People and deal with them that way, turn to page 117.

82 The mysterious alien leads you away from the packed refugees halls and into a maintenance corridor. There he stops.

"What is it you wanted to tell me?" you ask, genuinely mystified now.

"Back on Coruscant, you were looking for Goshan the Drak, weren't you?"

"I think you're mistaken," you tell the blue-skinned alien. "I found who I was looking for, and it wasn't Goshan the Drak."

It is then that you remember. Goshan the Drak was one of the characters mentioned by the Klatooinian enforcers you met on the door of the Outlander Club, down in the planet-city's underlevels.

"Oh, I know who you mean now," you begin, "but –"

The alien abruptly slams his hand against a control switch next to him, opening a panel in the wall behind you.

"Well now you've found him," he says with an angry snarl, and before you know what's going on, he pushes you through the open hatch.

You drop down a vertical chute into a stinking pile of rubbish. Picking yourself up, you find yourself wading through a rusty soup of waste oil and reeking food waste. You are just wondering how you are going to get back up the chute and out of the rubbish dump when somewhere a distant klaxon starts to sound and the pit you are in is washed by flashing amber lights.

An airlock yawns open and you are sucked out into the void of space along with the rest of the rubbish. Your adventure ends here, in the freezing, airless depths of space.

THE END

84 "It is vitally important that I enter the Senate," you say urgently.

"What is your business here?" the guard asks, his eyes and his rifle not moving from you for a moment.

"I am here on behalf of Master Shaak Ti of the Jedi Temple to make sure that Chancellor Palpatine makes it to safety."

"But the Senate isn't in session," he explains. "I expect you'll find the Chancellor in his private offices, if he hasn't left the building already."

It is certainly a possibility that Chancellor Palpatine is already safe, but you cannot neglect the task Shaak Ti has entrusted to you. You cannot leave until you have made sure that the Chancellor is no longer inside the Senate.

Turn to page 106.

85 The starfighter's lasers cannons pound your LAAT/i, the gunship's superficial armour failing under such an intense barrage. Although the gunners shoot back it is too little, too late. The conniving bounty hunter's ruse has worked.

Your gunship drops out of the sky in a terminal dive, plummeting towards the lake of molten metal that lies at the heart of an automated manufactory. You feel the unbearable inferno heat of the fiery lake increasing as the gunship drops lower. No one is going to walk away from this landing. Your adventure is over and Vogg Barakk has escaped.

THE END

86 With the freighter losing height by the second, it is a close run thing but you nevertheless manage to pilot the floundering vessel beyond the Senatorial district and into the industrialized zone known to all as the Works.

It is a place of abandoned self-maintaining factories, gangs of smugglers and uncontrolled power surges. You are looking for somewhere safe to land when the freighter becomes the target of one of these deadly ion bursts. You lose all power, and all control, in an instant.

The freighter drops out of the sky into the structure of a derelict waste-processing plant, its engine power core detonating moments after impact. You cannot survive such a cataclysmic explosion.

You may have saved the Senate and the Chancellor, but in the end you couldn't save yourself.

THE END

88 The former monastery is now a heavily-fortified citadel. Its towers and domes bristle with surveillance points and weapons emplacements, with many trained on the approach to the main gate. Deflector shields and a dissipation grid buried within the palace's thick walls protect it from enemy fire and make it all but impregnable. So how, exactly, are you going to get inside without being discovered or getting yourself shot?

After spending some time examining the outer walls of the palace from afar, whilst trying to avoid being spotted by Jabba's lookouts, you think you have found not one, but two hidden ways into the alien gangster's lair.

One looks like an old looters' tunnel. Although it is possible that it is actually the entrance to the den of some kind of desert-dwelling animal. It starts some distance away, out of sight of the main gate, and looks like it is travelling in the right direction. The other is a tunnel that appears to have been dug by the Jawas that have made the extensive junkyard behind the palace their home.

If you want to enter via the looters' tunnel, turn to page 112.

If you want to gain entry using the tunnel dug by the Jawas, turn to page 60.

If you want to use neither of these tunnels and now want to seek a formal audience with Jabba instead, turn to page 144.

89 You grovel before the Wookiees, and even though you don't speak their language you do your very best to make it plain how embarrassed you are and apologise for any inconvenience you may have caused them. It was the wise thing to do. The Wookiees back down too, their angry roars becoming guttural growls of inquiry. The Kashyyyk delegates then stride past you, allowing you to continue on your way.

As you are rounding another corner, still following your path to the turbo-lift to Palpatine's private quarters, you encounter the Chancellor and his closest confidantes, approaching from the other direction, accompanied by his personal Red Guard.

"Padawan?" the Chancellor says, registering the look of relief in your face. "What is the meaning of this?"

"We must evacuate," you explain, hardly able to believe that you – a humble Padawan learner – are addressing the supreme Chancellor of the Galactic Senate. "The whole Senate is in danger; you must leave immediately, Chancellor. I have been sent to get you to safety by my Master, Shaak Ti of the Jedi Temple."

"Then lead the way, young Padawan," Chancellor Palpatine instructs you.

You waste no time in leading Palpatine and his advisors along the twisting corridors of the Senate and out of the building.

Waiting for the Chancellor outside on the landing pad is his personal shuttle, already firing up its engines, and with its ramp down, ready to carry him to safety. A myriad of other shuttle craft are lifting off from the docking platform carrying those on-board out of harm's way.

Glancing up at the crystal clear blue sky you can see the Trandoshan freighter quite clearly now as it closes on the Senate. It is so close that you wonder if you can make it to safety in time yourself, before it crashes into the mushroom-shaped dome of the Galactic Senate.

And then the snub nose of the vessel rises sharply and the plummeting freighter clears the Senate, the subsonic thrumming of its engines almost shaking you off your feet – but at least you are still alive. The Senate has been saved.

Suddenly Commander Fox is there at your side, following your gaze as a flight of fire-suppression ships guides the freighter towards a suitable landing site.

"The Senate is safe!" you gasp.

"You said it, Padawan," Commander Fox replies, "and we have Trin'dal Vek to thank for it. She sure is some Jedi," he says, whistles admiringly.

And you completed your mission for Master Ti by making sure that Chancellor Palpatine got out safely too. You are just as much of a hero as Trin'dal Vek.

Turn to page 11.

91 Turning right, you make your way cautiously along the narrow passageway. On reaching the T-junction you can hear the hubbub of voices and the scuffle of movement drifting to you from your left. You suspect that you are close to Jabba the Hutt's audience chamber.

Breathing deeply, in an effort to control your quickening heart-rate, you creep along the passageway, on the lookout for anyone approaching you from either behind or ahead.

Light spills into the gloomy tunnel from a chamber ahead and you peer through an archway into Jabba the crime lord's throne room. What you see there makes your heart race all the faster.

On one side of the chamber, the huge slug-like amphibian is reclining on a dais. But the sight of the bloated crime lord isn't what has attracted your attention and driven you into such a state of agitation. It is the figure standing before him that has done that – the sworn enemy of the Jedi, the Dark Acolyte Asajj Ventress herself!

As you watch, Ventress draws her twin lightsabers. What is Ventress doing? Is she here to kill the crime lord? Is Jabba in danger? If you are to find out what's going on here, you're going to need him alive.

If you want to charge in, igniting your own lightsaber as you do so, ready to defend the Hutt, turn to page 40.

If you want to remain where you are hidden, and simply watch and wait, turn to page 63.

92 The autopilot has been engaged and locked with an encrypted code. You will need to crack this code if you are to disengage the navicom, unlock the freighter's controls and alter the vessel's course. But cracking the code isn't going to be easy and time is running out fast. It would be a lot easier, of course, with the help of an astromech droid.

If R2-X4 is accompanying you, turn to page 140.

If there is no droid with you, click on box B on screen and type code word NAVICOM or turn to page 178.

93 You were right to prepare to defend yourself. Screaming like a Corellian banshee bird, the Rattatakan comes at you with one blazing red lightsaber in each hand. You parry one strike then the next, but Ventress is relentless and it is all you can do to keep your balance on the gangplank whilst deflecting her blows.

With you unable to break through her whirling attacks and make a strike of your own against her, Ventress is steadly pushing you back towards the end of the gangplank. In a moment it won't matter whether you can beat her in battle or not as you'll simply drop off the end into the monster's mouth and become supper for the Sarlacc.

You are going to have to try something a little different, and fast.

If you want to summon all your reserves of energy and take the fight to Ventress, click box M on screen and type code word DUEL.

If you want to try to trick her with a feint, turn to page 69.

If you want to try to leap over Ventress to get to the skiff-ward end of the gangplank, turn to page 158.

94 Not wanting to risk losing one of the valuable gunships to the raging robot, you order the LAAT/is out of the colossal droid's way. But as the gunships take evasive action to avoid colliding with the monstrous machine, the squadron veers close to the gas-gushing chimneys of an ore-processing plant. The jet wash of the trailing gunship ignites a pocket of flammable gas that spurts from one of the chimneys.

There is nothing you can do but watch in appalled horror from your LAAT/i as the gunship bringing up the rear disappears in the midst of a rapidly expanding fireball, and doesn't reappear. It is with a heavy heart that you realize there is nothing you can do to help the clones trapped on-board, but they will be avenged if you can catch the bounty hunter.

And so it is that only two gunships are there to meet with Vogg Barakk as he emerges from the wasteland of the dead zone.

Turn to page 107.

95 You throw yourself behind a workbench laden with hyperdrive parts as a volley of laser-fire rips through the side of the hangar. Searing laser blasts shatter windows and smack into the spare parts lying on the bench above you. The Toydarian isn't so lucky. The blue-skinned alien drops on to the floor of the hangar and doesn't move again.

As the laser-fire subsides, you risk a glance over the top of the bench in time to see a hovering ASN-class droid departing the scene of the crime. Someone sent that droid to silence the Toydarian and stop your only lead from revealing what you need to know. The only way to find out who that was, and still have a chance of getting to the bottom of this mystery, is to pursue the droid and let it lead you back to its master.

Turn to page 56.

96 Bringing the starfighter in close, you open fire with the craft's full complement of dual laser cannons. When the smoke and flame clears you see that the freighter is still there; all you have managed to do is blast a section of metal plate free from the side of the vessel.

This wrecked panel whickers towards you. You jink the starfighter to starboard to avoid a head-on collision with the debris but the hurtling plate hits the astromech, cleanly removing the top of the droid in a welter of sparks.

That was a close call – one that was too close for comfort!

Turn to page 157.

97 You are a student of the Jedi Temple. You're sure you can deal with whoever is behind all this just as well on your own as you could with the clones' help. You get the taxi driver to drop you off as close to the disused refinery as he dares and, having settled the fare, leap out.

Lightsaber in hand, you scamper up to the building. It is eerily quiet; the only sounds you can hear are the venting of steam and exhaust fumes from distant manufactory chimneys. Keeping a wary eye out for any signs of life – human or otherwise – you creep into the gloomy shadows beneath the refinery.

The laser tripwire-beam is invisible to the naked eye and so you know nothing of the danger you are in until you block the beam and trigger the explosives planted within the foundations of the building to protect the villain from any unwanted intrusions. The sound of the bombs touching off is the last thing you ever hear. Your adventure ends here as your body is atomised by the force of the explosion.

THE END

98 You reach the entrance to the shadowy tunnels without incident. You peer into the mouth of the nearest tunnel. It is pitch black in there, but it could lead to a way up and out of this forgotten underworld.

Igniting the blade of your lightsaber to provide you with a source of illumination, and taking a deep breath, you set off into the gloom. But unfortunately, unknown to you, the tunnels are home to the ghoulish Cthons. These half-human creatures are nearly blind, dwelling in near-permanent darkness, but their other senses compensate in ways you could never imagine.

As you travel deeper and deeper into their territory, a pack of Cthon hunters carefully surrounds you. When they are all in place, and with you still unaware of their skulking presence, they spring their trap.

In a moment you are trussed up in their electroshock nets. You are carried away to their cave-like lair barely conscious, there to be made into the main course of a great celebratory feast. Your adventure ends here in a most gruesome fashion.

THE END

99 Taking a deep breath, wondering if you've really made the right decision, you crouch before Jabba's throne-dais and lay your lightsaber on the ground in front of him.

"Take this as a sign of not only my word but also of the trust the Jedi and the Hutt clan share," you say eloquently, bowing your head whilst still on bended knee before the dais.

This is all the proof Jabba needs.

At their lord's command Gamorrean guards step forward to take the Dark Acolyte prisoner, but Ventress is too quick for them. Back-flipping over the heads of the advancing Gamorreans, she hurtles out of the throne room and away into the depths of the palace.

You would chase after her yourself, but you are exhausted after all that you have been through and are in no fit state to start chasing anyone at the moment. It's possible that Jabba's guards will catch up with the assassin before she escapes from the citadel and makes it to the safety of the outside world – and her waiting speeder, no doubt – but you suspect that the Republic and the Jedi haven't heard the last of Asajj Ventress.

But at least you now understand who was really behind the attack on the Senate on Coruscant. One of those loyal to Count Dooku and the Separatists hired Vogg Barakk to initiate the attack on the Senate – possibly Ventress herself or maybe even Ziro the Hutt, a known, and currently imprisoned, Separatist collaborator – laying a false trail that would make the Republic and the Jedi believe that Jabba was responsible for the atrocity. At the same time Asajj Ventress travelled to Tatooine to manipulate Jabba into believing that the Jedi were trying to get him out of the way.

One way or another, Count Dooku's agents hoped to sow the seeds of discontent which, at best, would have the defenders of the Republic tying up resources they could ill afford to waste, and which at worst could quite easily have resulted in the Hutt clan going to war with the Republic. With the Republic then fighting a war on two fronts, and having to spread its forces too thinly, the CIS would succeed in their conquest of the galaxy and all would fall to the droid armies of the Separatists.

But by your actions, you have ensured that that will never happen and when you finally return to Master Ti at the Jedi Temple, you will be rightly celebrated as one of the heroes of the Clone Wars.

Congratulations, Padawan. We'll make a Jedi knight of you yet!

THE END

102   You run at the rancor, your lightsaber raised high above your head in both hands, hoping to deal with the distraction of Jabba's pet before you have to face Ventress in battle. It is then that you see a way to escape from the monster, the pit and Count Dooku's favoured agent, all at the same time.

The bellowing rancor makes a grab for you, but its huge claws close on empty air as, at the last possible moment, you launch yourself into the air in a death-defying somersault.

You land on its arm and scramble up to its shoulders. From there, you vault upwards, reaching for the grilled trapdoor above your head.

Holding on to a metal strut with one hand, you cut yourself a hole in the grille with your lightsaber and clamber through.

Howling in frustration at having been robbed of its prize, the captive rancor turns on Ventress. You catch a glimpse of the Dark Acolyte as she backs away fearfully from the advancing monster.

"You can't leave me here!" she screams at you, fear writ large in her snake-like eyes. "Help me, Jedi. Be merciful. Get me out of here!"

She fixes you with an imploring stare and reaches out a hand to you even as the rancor bears down on her, claws flailing.

If you want to help Asajj Ventress out of the rancor pit, turn to page 172.

If you would rather leave her to her fate, turn to page 132.

103 It is said that if you want to know about anything that's happening on Coruscant the best place to go is Dexter's Diner. Located far from the more fashionable eateries on Coruscant, lying within one of the planet's many business and manufacturing districts, it is an unassuming place, run by the four-armed Besalisk Dexter Jettster. Thanks to a chequered past with oil-harvesting crews across the galaxy, many of Dexter's shady associates from the past look him out, along with a newer crowd of regulars, to plumb his amazing memory or to make use of one of his many, and diverse, contacts.

So it is that you find yourself disembarking from a civilian airbus, pushing open the door and stepping into Dexter's Diner in search of information.

A pretty blonde-haired waitress catches sight of you and, acknowledging you with a cheery smile, starts to move towards you and offer you a menu. However, before she can cross the diner she is beaten to it by an antique droid waitress that trundles over to you on her unipod arrangement drive system. The human waitress's face falls and she goes back to wiping the table she was clearing.

"Hello there," she says chirpily. "And what can I get for you today?"

If you want to order something from the menu, turn to page 181.

If you want to cut the chit-chat and demand to speak with Dexter straight away, turn to page 162.

104 The sandcrawler and its crew are busy salvaging the wreckage of a downed cruiser, working into the deepening dusk under the powerful arc lights mounted to the hull of the monolithic machine.

The Jawas quickly surround your landspeeder, poking at it while jabbering to themselves excitedly.

The Jawas eventually make themselves understood – thanks in part to a protocol droid they recovered from another wrecked craft – and make it clear that in exchange for your landspeeder they will take you wherever you want to go, which is Jabba's Palace.

If you want to accept the Jawas' offer, turn to page 15.

If you decline and turn your landspeeder around, choosing to take an alternative route to Jabba's Palace over the Northern Dune Sea, turn to page 126.

105 As soon as you mention the name Goshan the Drak, the Klatooinians draw their blasters, pointing them straight at you.

"What do you want with that no good, low-life slythmonger?" the first demands, waving his blaster around dangerously.

You stammer as you try to think of a suitable reply. You had no idea that this Goshan character was a known criminal; if you had, you would never have dared mention his name. Now these self-proclaimed protectors of Coruscant's underlevels are convinced you're connected with him.

"You're under arrest," the enforcer says.

"We're taking you in for questioning," says his partner. "And I wouldn't even think about resisting either," the Klatooinian warns you.

If you want to activate your lightsaber and show the enforcers who it is they're really dealing with, turn to page 141.

If you would rather go quietly, turn to page 167.

106 You head for Palpatine's private offices without further delay. You are on the final approach to his chamber when you run into one of Commander Fox's Coruscant Guard.

"What are you doing, Padawan?" he demands. "Everyone's been evacuated from this area. You should get out too, while there's still time."

"But I have to make sure that the Chancellor is safe," you explain.

"There's no time. That freighter's going to hit any second now. I'd save yourself while you still can." And with that he runs past you back up the corridor.

Time is indeed running out, so what are you going to do?

If you want to persist with your mission to save the Chancellor, turn to page 170.

If you would rather save yourself, while you still can, turn to 148.

107 And then the Republic gunships are bearing down on Vogg Barakk's craft again, but the bounty hunter is still determined to get away. You are steadily closing the gap between yourselves and the starfighter when the bounty hunter veers sharply to port taking you over a disused chemical waste processing plant.

This whole area is covered by a fog of toxic gas that has effectively turned the very atmosphere here into a corrosive agent. The bounty hunter is taking a huge risk by entering this area himself as the reactants suspended in the air could cause catastrophic damage to his repulsor engines.

If you want to keep pursuing the felon, turn to page 128.

If you would rather direct the gunship's pilot to skirt around this toxic zone, in the hope of catching up with the bounty hunter on the other side, turn to page 54.

108 Fortunately your craft makes it through to the other side of the toxic zone. Now that the gunship's sensor arrays are working properly again and are no longer being dampened by the pollutant cloud, proximity alarms start to sound as the bounty hunter's starfighter swoops down out of the smoggy sky above you, like some savage alien bird of prey, all guns blazing.

If yours is the only gunship left after your perilous journey through the Works, turn to page 85.

If there is at least one other LAAT/i still in the air with you, turn to page 42.

109 Even as you reach for your lightsaber, the stocky Gamorreans make a grab for you. Although you struggle against them, Jabba's palace guard have the status they do precisely because they are very strong and tough.

There is little you can do as the Gamorreans take you prisoner, dragging you off between them into the depths of the citadel, to deal with you as they deal with all trespassers.

Turn to page 151.

110 Grasping the con-stick, you pull back as you alter the pitch of the craft with a control panel to your left.

With the freighter's engines screaming in protest and the ship shaking so hard around you that you fear that it might actually shake itself apart, the snub nose of the freighter slowly begins to rise, as the Senate fills the view shield in front of you.

For a moment, all you can see is the curving dome of the Senate building and then there is sky and clouds above you again, and you are clear.

You give a whoop of joy, even though you're the only person there to hear it, but it feels great just the same.

Then you become aware of another sound – a blaring klaxon noise – that twists your stomach into a nauseous knot. The freighter's engines are failing; no doubt one last nasty surprise left behind by whoever is responsible for the attack on the Galactic Senate.

Without sufficient power you won't be able to pilot the ship into space so you are going to have to put it down somewhere on the ground and fast; somewhere where it can't cause anyone else any harm.

You could try putting the freighter down in the virtually uninhabited Works district, which lies adjacent to the Senate district, or you could risk putting the vessel down on a landing platform nearby.

If you want to try to reach the Works before attempting to land the craft, turn to page 86.

If you don't want to risk leaving it so long and would rather put the freighter down somewhere closer, turn to page 58.

112 The hand-dug tunnel is so small that you are forced to crawl along it on your hands and knees. It rises and falls as you get deeper. You rather unnervingly pass a pile of mouldering bones that look like they belong to someone who once tried to steal from Jabba the Hutt and who died in the attempt. The bones show signs of having been gnawed . . .

Fortunately you make it to the end of the tunnel unscathed and emerge from it to discover, to your delight, that it has taken you to precisely where you wanted to go – into the heart of Jabba the Hutt's lair!

You are standing in a sculpted passageway somewhere beneath the foundations of the ancient B'omarr monastery, constructed long before Jabba the Hutt remade the place as his own pleasure palace. The air down here is hot and stuffy and thick with cooking smells.

The corridor is empty, ending to both left and right at a junction with another passageway. But in which direction lies Jabba's throne room?

If you want to go right, turn to page 91.

If you want to head left, turn to page 50.

113 Jumping into the pilot's seat of the drag racer-style airspeeder, you thumb the ignition trigger and press down hard on the accelerator with your foot. The propulsion gives a juddering cough and then, with a purring roar, the speeder lurches into the air.

Gunning the throttle you cajole the airspeeder up to its top speed and, aiming directly at the distant speck in the Coruscant sky, pilot the craft towards the out-of-control freighter.

In no time at all, it seems, you are bringing the airspeeder in over the freighter. You battle the craft's controls, as it becomes caught in the treacherous air currents created by the freighter's mass, while plunging through the atmosphere of the planet.

There is a heart-stopping moment when you think you are about to lose the airspeeder, as it becomes trapped in the whirling vortex of a slipstream, and then you are touching down on top of the freighter. You engage its magna-locks, securing the airspeeder to the hull.

Clinging on to whatever handholds the outside of the freighter affords you and keeping your head down against the buffeting wind, you pull yourself towards the nearest maintenance hatch.

Activating your lightsaber, you force the hatch open with its blazing energy blade and then drop into the dark interior of the freighter. Having taken a moment to orientate yourself, you head for the flight deck.

Turn to page 20.

114 Taking the time to explain to the Toydarian - whose name you discover is Bhuto - the situation you are in and about the attack on the Senate, you slowly but surely gain his trust.

"I had no idea!" he grunts, appalled, when you tell him how the freighter was set on a collision course with the Senate. "I would never have signed the lease agreement if I had known that that was what he had in mind," Bhuto goes on anxiously. "But you can't pin anything on me, hmm?"

"And I wouldn't want to," you reassure him. "But to help me, if you could just give me a name, the Jedi and the Coruscant Guard would be most grateful."

The Toydarian flits over to a table laden with spare parts – pieces of an ion drive pre-accelerator and swoop bike steering vanes – and starts flicking through a pile of oil-stained paperwork.

"Here it is," he says at last, sounding embarrassed but still desperate to disassociate himself from any Republic-threatening crime. "I knew there was something suspicious about him, but not so suspicious of course that I told him to get out straight away, you understand, hmm?"

"And the name?" you say, focusing his attention back to the matter in hand.

"Vogg Barakk," Bhuto says. "A bounty hunter; a Snivvian. Word is he's hiding out in the Works, along with that gang of Pacithhip smugglers."

You leave the haulier's beaming from ear to ear, knowing that the vital information you need to help resolve the crisis on Coruscant is in your grasp.

Turn to page 186.

116 Although it seems to go against every Jedi instinct you have, to willingly give up your lightsaber, these are desperate times, and desperate times call for desperate measures . . .

Opening your hand, you let go of the weapon, which drops into the pit, there to be snapped out of the air by the grotesque beaked tongue of the Sarlacc and swallowed. It is lost to you forever now, but at least you have two free hands with which to grasp the gangplank.

"You think that will save you, fool?" Ventress sneers as she leans out over the precipice, bending towards you with her lightsabers still in her hands, and still lit. You are completely exposed as she lunges for you with both blades.

Turn to page 142.

117 Dismounting from the dewback, you leave it behind to negotiate the rugged cliffs on foot, although in places you have to rely on your hands as well to traverse a path that is near-vertical in places. But you at last reach the top of the cliff, and the Tusken raider's hiding place – only the sniper isn't the only one lying in wait there; there's a whole gang of them.

Igniting your lightsaber once more, you leap into battle, whirling about you with your blade like a true Jedi knight. The disorganized Tusken don't stand a chance.

With the way through the hills now clear, Harlon Nayl's merchant caravan is safe to proceed on its way.

Eventually you leave the caravan behind, your duties as bodyguard discharged, proceeding again on foot to make the last leg of your journey alone, towards the palace of Jabba the Hutt.

Click box I on screen and type code word PALACE or turn to page 180.

118 You cling on to the droid for dear life as it climbs higher and higher between the sky-scraper canyons of Coruscant, not daring to let go, convinced that you could never survive a fall from such a height — even with your renowned Jedi powers.

But the droid continues to crackle and spit sparks of electricity from its outer casing until in a sudden burst of bright light, it electrifies the whole hull, hitting you with a massive jolt of energy.

You are thrown from the droid by the force of the discharge. Electrocuted, you drop senseless down through the speeding lanes of Coruscant traffic, down through the upper city, down into the underlevels again. As you plummet into the dark depths of the planet-city you lose consciousness . . .

Turn to page 45.

119 Past the huge pile of scrap metal thrown out from the palace, lies the opening of the Jawas' secret tunnel. You have to stoop as you proceed along it, those who dug it out of the hillside being considerably shorter than the average human, and use the flickering blue blade of your activated lightsaber to illuminate your way onwards.

After creeping about in near-darkness, bent almost double for nearly an hour as you follow the twists and turns of the passageway, you finally see a light at the end of the tunnel.

You ease open a grilled vent and clamber through it into a gloomy subterranean corridor formed from a series of stone-cut archways. A musty atmosphere permeates the place and you can hear the murmur of what sounds like burbling cantina music echoing along the corridor from somewhere else deep within the citadel.

Hearing a gruff grunting sound you duck into cover behind a pillar as a pair of Jabba's brutish, green-skinned Gamorrean guards round the bend of the passageway ahead of you, grim-looking vibro-lances in hand. You were only just in time but fortunately they didn't see you – and haven't smelt you either – and so trudge straight past your hiding place.

Just when you think it's safe to move on you hear a sharp chattering behind you and you look back up the tunnel to see a pair of hooded Jawa faces peering out of the still open vent-grille. Their shrill jabbering voices alert the dull-witted Gamorreans who turn around in time to see you trying to make your getaway.

But even as you prepare to defend yourself with your glowing lightsaber, another pair of pug-faced Gamorreans appears from the other end of the dusty passageway and you find yourself surrounded.

You are about to engage the first of the ugly creatures in single combat when a thought strikes you. You have come here to find out whether Jabba the Hutt really was behind the attack on the Senate on Coruscant, and face to face might be the best way. So it is that you deactivate your lightsaber and put up your hands in surrender, ready for the Gamorrean guards to take you into custody.

Turn to page 151.

121 "I don't know what this is about, but I'm not going anywhere with you," you tell the alien bluntly.

"So be it," he says. "Then we'll settle things right here and now."

The strange, blue-faced alien abruptly drops his food tray and pulls a blaster from within his robes. Those people standing nearby quickly move away from you, yelping with surprise.

"Because of you I had to leave behind a very lucrative trade in the black market on Coruscant. Had to leave in a hurry, with barely a credit to my name," he whines, gesticulating wildly with his weapon. His anger at whatever slight he believes you have caused him is making him behave in a totally irrational way. He's gone absolutely crazy!

This individual must be Goshan, a two-bit, low-life slythmonger who peddled his evil trade in the underlevels of Coruscant, and if you don't want to wind up being shot dead by him, you are going to have to act fast.

If you want to try to overcome this dangerous individual using your Jedi mind powers, turn to page 145.

If you would rather use your lightsaber to engage in some aggressive negotiations with the alien slythmonger, turn to page 171.

122 "But Master, I am better than this," you begin. "So I made one lousy mistake. I'm not going to let that hold me back. I am a good Jedi. But I could be a great Jedi. Give me the chance and I'll prove it to you."

Shaak Ti looks suddenly taken aback. "I have never heard you speak like this before, Padawan. Such disobedience and impudence are not becoming of a Jedi. Your attitude tells me that there is more – dare I say it? – of the dark side about you than the Jedi. You have disgraced yourself. I cannot permit you to continue as a member of the Jedi Order."

You cannot quite believe what you are hearing. Can Shaak Ti really mean what she is saying? It hardly seems credible.

"Give me your lightsaber," she says.

Slowly, in a state of shock, you unhook your lightsaber from the belt of your robe and place it into Master Ti's open palm. "You are expelled from the Order," she says solemnly, pronouncing sentence. "Never darken the door of the Temple again." She then turns on her heel and marches away from you.

You are left feeling hollow and empty, but you have no one to blame but yourself. All your hopes for a glorious future as a Jedi Knight of the Galactic Republic have been dashed. Your adventure is over.

THE END

123 "You see, my lord," Ventress says addressing Jabba, "this was the Jedi's plan all along, to send an assassin to kill you, just as I warned you they would."

You suspect that the Dark Acolyte must have been following your movements for some time now.

"This one's presence here, within your own palace, is all the proof you need that the Jedi are plotting against you," she goes on, spreading more of her malicious lies with every word she speaks. "They do not trust you, O great and mighty Jabba, and I fear they want to remove you, to get you out of the way so that they might proceed with their nefarious plans."

In response to this outrageous claim, a great rumbling growl rises from deep within Jabba's throat as he passes judgement on you.

Turn to page 18.

124 Vogg Barakk spends most of the journey in shameful silence — and security bracelets — with you keeping a close watch over him in the main cabin of the gunship.

But as your LAAT/i comes in to land, in the shadow of the still-standing Galactic Senate building, the bounty hunter starts to look uncomfortable and fidgets nervously.

"You expect me to talk, do you?" he says, making a poor effort of challenging your authority as a representative of the Jedi Order.

"I would certainly suggest you cooperate fully with our investigation and answer any questions my Master Shaak Ti puts to you," you tell the bounty hunter. It is all you can do to restrain your anger after what he tried to do to the Senate and the Chancellor, and what he's effectively put you through since. "After you attempted to assassinate Chancellor Palpatine, I think you'll find that you are the most wanted criminal on Coruscant right now."

A defeated look enters his eyes and his shoulders sag. "The one you really want is the Hutt," he says mysteriously.

"The Hutt?" you say.

"That's who hired me to do the job," Barakk explains. "Jabba the Hutt."

Turn to 174.

125 After a tedious but uneventful trip – a small mercy for which you are suitably grateful – the refugee ship drops out of hyperspace and enters the Tatooine system. The planet appears as a dusty yellow ball, suspended in the black depths of the void.

In no time at all it seems, after your long voyage, the vessel is battling the buffeting winds of the planet's atmosphere and coming in to land at Mos Espa, one of the planet's largest spaceports.

Turn to page 35.

126 Leaving the fractured chasms behind, you pilot the humming landspeeder out of the shadow of the Great Mesa highlands and over the wind-rippled sands of the Northern Dune Sea.

You crest the rise of a particularly large hill of sand and come face to snout with a monstrous reptile that was basking in the last rays of Tatooine's sinking suns, before setting out to hunt in the cool of the night. It must be at least fifty metres long, with a huge horned head the same size as your landspeeder.

You have run into various different monsters during missions Shaak Ti carried out on behalf of the Jedi Temple but you have never encountered anything as ferocious and as dangerous as a fully grown krayt dragon. Unfortunately, you have now . . .

As the huge reptile bellows its challenge, you are forced to think fast to work out how to deal with the monster.

If you want to put your foot down and ram the dragon with the landspeeder, turn to 153.

If you want to go up against the hungry monster with your lightsaber, turn to page 169.

127 You sprint out of the Senate and on to the docking skirt, with the Red Guard in tow, in time to see Chancellor Palpatine and his party boarding the Chancellor's personal escape shuttle.

Then you catch sight of Master Ti and Senator Amidala waiting anxiously at the foot of a ramp of another shuttle craft ready for take-off. Seeing you, Master Ti calls out, "Have no fear, Padawan, the Chancellor is safe. And it is time we were away as well."

As you sprint across the landing pad towards the hovering shuttle you dare a glance at the sky. What you see there fills you with dread. The Trandoshan freighter is clearly visible now as it closes on the Senate.

Suddenly, the vessel changes course, the snub nose of the vessel rising sharply and you feel relief wash through you as the freighter clears the Senate with a sonic boom. You watch as the freighter, now being accompanied by a flight of fire-suppression ships, heads off towards a safe landing site.

"The Senate is safe!" you gasp.

"Yes, Padawan," Master Shaak Ti says, in that calm way of hers, "and we have Trin'dal Vek to thank for it. That one is a true Jedi in the making. As are you," she adds, seeing your face fall momentarily in disappointment. "You attempted to complete your mission to the very best of your ability. No teacher can ask more of a student."

Turn to page 11.

128 The clone pilots courageously take the gunships into the toxic smog, without a thought for their own safety, loyally obeying your commands. You immediately lose sight of the bounty hunter's ship through the pollutant mist, the contaminated atmosphere even interfering with your ship's instruments.

Your pilot slows to half speed, having to rely on his own senses and nothing else to navigate his way through the cloud. Tensely you watch the orangey-green smog through the cockpit canopy for any sign of movement from behind the pilot's position.

You suddenly hear a dull boom from somewhere off the gunship's starboard bow and the toxic fog becomes suffused with bright light. The crackling comm signal from the gunship on your right wing cuts off completely to be replaced by static. A LAAT/i has been claimed by the treacherous toxic gas cloud.

Turn to page 108.

129 The three gunships swoop down in formation towards the droid, and open fire with their massed battery of composite-beam laser turrets. The corroded exterior-plating of the construction droid affords it little protection in the face of such an attack.

As the lifter droid topples into the ruins of the starship factory, its internal chambers ablaze, all three LAAT/i gunships rocket through the cloud of smoke rising into the infernal sky above the Works and continue on their way towards their rendezvous with the bounty hunter's starfighter.

Turn to page 107.

130 Setting about your task immediately you rush into the Senate building, passing between the towering statues of the Republic's Core World founders that adorn the entrance concourse, as Commander Fox's clones hurry in alongside you.

Entering the cool shaded corridors of the building's interior, you are welcomed by the wailing of an alarm bell warning the Senators and their entourages to evacuate immediately. You fight the tide of intergalactic species rushing to escape the Senate as you struggle to enter it.

As you dodge the evacuating Senators and their retinues – myriad life-forms representing the thousands of sentient species distributed across the galaxy – you run past a clone trooper who calls out, "Padawan, please wait!"

If you want to stop and listen to what the trooper has to say, click box 0 on screen and type code word TROOPER, or turn to page 154.

If you think that your mission is too urgent, turn to page 78.

131 After you have been waiting for almost two hours, the portly Besalisk cook finally emerges from the kitchen and, wiping his hands on his greasy apron, approaches your window seat.

"I hear you wanted to see me," he says gruffly, his nose-whiskers twitching as he studies you with a beady eye.

You hurriedly tell Dexter about the attack on the Senate and the attempt on Chancellor Palpatine's life.

"I don't know anything about that," he says bluntly. "You'd do better to ask around at the Outlander Club, in the Uscru entertainment district." And with that the Besalisk turns and goes back to his busy kitchen.

You leave Dexter's Diner without further delay.

Turn to page 16.

132 Asajj Ventress cannot be trusted and does not deserve your assistance. She would only turn it against you somehow even if you did help her. Leaving her to her fate in the pit below, you stagger away from the trapdoor to come before Jabba the Hutt once more.

"My lord Jabba," you manage through gasping breaths, "begging your indulgence, you will see that I have defeated my accuser and proven my innocence to you."

A great amphibian croaking sound belches from the Hutt's quivering body. Is he furious? Is he going to have you killed where you stand?

And then you realize that Jabba is laughing. But what can he possibly find so funny at a time like this? It is then that you get the uncomfortable feeling that someone is watching you with intent interest.

You slowly turn your head to see Asajj Ventress standing with her legs straddling the hole you cut in the grilled trapdoor. She too has managed to escape from the pit, without your help.

"So you defeated me, did you?" she says with mocking scorn. "See how the Jedi's true intentions are revealed, my lord Jabba. See how the Jedi comes before you now, lightsaber drawn."

It is only then that you realize that your lightsaber is indeed still in your hand, its blue blade alive with crackling energy.

The crime lord's laughter abruptly stops.

"His greatness, the mighty Jabba, commands," TC-70 translates as his master croaks out another declaration in Huttese, "that you drop your weapon."

Can he be serious, when Asajj Ventress is standing right behind you with her twin lightsabers drawn as well?

If you want to do as Jabba commands and lay down your lightsaber before Jabba's dais, turn to page 99.

If you want to keep a tight hold of your weapon, turn to page 47.

134 Having visited the Senate on a number of occasions with Master Ti, running errands for the Jedi Council, you know the way to the Senate Rotunda itself. You dodge past Kel Dor delegates and a gaggle of Sy Myrthians, all desperate to escape the building having heard the evac alarm.

As you are approaching the Senate Chamber, a guard wearing the striking blue robes and high-plumed helm of the Senate Guard steps into your path. His uniform is more a symbol of the Senate's supreme authority and power than a functional protective suit but the stun rifle slung over his shoulder looks like it could still cause you some pain.

"Halt!" he commands, swinging the rifle from his shoulder and into his hands. "No one may enter the Senate Chamber. The building is being evacuated."

The guard fixes you with a purposeful stare, his eyes the same striking ultramarine as his robes. He does not look like the sort of man who will be easily persuaded to change his mind.

If you want to try to persuade the guard to let you enter the Senate chamber, turn to page 84.

If you want to double back and then find a way to sneak past the guard when he's not looking, turn to page 53.

135 By the time you make planet-fall on Tatooine, at the Mos Espa spaceport, you discover just how fast the news of your presence on-board the refugee ship has travelled.

You step down from the passenger ramp from the chilled interior of the mass transporter and into the baking heat of Tatooine's twin suns to find a metal-cased droid waiting there to greet you.

"I am protocol droid TC-70 and I am here on behalf of the great Jabba the Hutt," the droid says, shuffling towards you over the sand-blown floor of the landing pad. "The mighty Jabba welcomes you to Tatooine and asks that you attend him at his palace forthwith. We have transport on standby to take you to him directly."

A personal summons from Jabba the Hutt; not every Padawan learner can claim to have had one of those.

If you want to accept the invitation and attend Jabba, turn to page 27.

If you would prefer to make your own way to Jabba's palace, and in your own good time, turn to page 35.

136 The protocol droid leads you deeper into the citadel, down flights of stairs and along musty corridors, to a room alive with light and sound and strange, exotic smells. And so you enter the throne room of Jabba the Hutt.

The mighty amphibian Hutts have controlled great swathes of space for thousands of years and Jabba's own Desilijic clan still controls trade routes in the Outer Rim. Ruthless and greedy, he sits at the centre of an extensive criminal empire and, as a result, all manner of alien pirates, mercenaries, corrupt galactic officials, entertainers and servants are drawn to his court.

A myriad of sparkling coloured lights reflect from the gleaming metal body of the droid, as it leads you into the throne room and before the raised dais on which squats the bloated slug-like amphibian that is Jabba the Hutt.

"The most gracious, the most compassionate Jabba the Hutt," the droid TC-70 says, with a wave of one gleaming silver hand.

"Greetings, mighty Jabba," you begin, bowing low before the alien crime lord, suddenly feeling very small and very alone.

The huge Hutt then says something in his own croaking language. It is a well known fact that he will only speak Huttese to visitors to his lair and so TC-70 sets to work translating for your benefit, so that you might hear the wisdom of the mighty Jabba.

"So," the protocol droid says, "Count Dooku's messenger was right;

the Jedi have sent an assassin to kill his lordship."

What is the meaning of this? What can Jabba be thinking?

"I beg your forgiveness, O mighty Jabba," you say, your mind racing, "but I do not understand what you mean? I haven't come here to kill you. I have been sent by my Master Shaak Ti to ask for your aid with a matter that has recently preoccupied us on Coruscant. Who is this messenger of Count Dooku's that has told you otherwise?" you ask. And then a horrible thought hits you.

"Is that so, Jedi?" says a sinister female voice dripping with malice, and in that instant your worst fears are confirmed.

You spin round to see the treacherous Asajj Ventress emerge from among the massed members of Jabba's court.

"If the Jedi Council wanted the great Jabba's help then why didn't they make contact themselves? Why send a lone, armed warrior?"

You have walked into a trap. Count Dooku's servant has obviously been sent here to spread lies about the Jedi to turn the powerful crime lord against the Republic. If Ventress were to succeed it could end with the Hutts declaring war on the Jedi and the Republic. If that were to happen, the clone armies of the Republic would soon find themselves having to fight a war on two fronts, against both the Confederacy of Independent Systems and the Hutt clan, and that could prove catastrophic for the galaxy.

You have to find some way to prove your innocence to the powerful gangster.

If you want to try to convince the Hutt that you are telling the truth and that Ventress can't be trusted, click box J on screen and type code word JABBA.

If you want to ask that you be allowed to prove your innocence through trial by combat against your accuser, turn to page 176.

139 "You rented out a freighter recently," you say to the Toydarian.

"Did I? What if I did, hmm?" the fluttering alien retorts defensively. "I hire out a lot of freighters. Who told you, hmm?"

"I know you want to tell me who you rented it to," you say, focusing your will on the alien and making a gesture of influence at the same time.

"Why would I want to do that?" the Toydarian asks, watching your hand movements with intense curiosity.

"You want to tell me," you repeat, trying to influence the alien telepathically.

"No I don't! I don't know what you're talking about," the hovering Toydarian snarls irritably. "Your Jedi mind tricks won't work on me. Now leave me alone, hmm? I've got work to do."

Unfortunately Toydarians, like the Hutt, are resistant to Jedi mind tricks.

Just as you are wondering what to do next, your heightened Jedi senses tell you that you are in danger. There is no sign of an attacker — yet — but you sense an attack is only moments away.

How will you react in response to this warning?

If you activate your lightsaber in readiness for battle, turn to page 156.

If you decide to take cover, turn to page 95.

140 As the rattling freighter continues to hurtle towards the rapidly-approaching Senate, R2-X4 trundles over to the navicom, extends a probe from inside itself and inserts it into an access port.

For a few tense seconds there is a series of clicks and hums as the droid's probe makes a series of rotations. Then you hear a click and a bleep as the autopilot disengages, and feel an excited surge of relief. But you and the Senate are not out of danger yet.

Turn to page 110.

141   You'll show these self-appointed law enforcers who really has the authority round here. Grabbing your lightsaber you whip it from your belt.

You barely have time to thumb the activation switch before the two Klatooinians gun you down where you stand.

Your adventure ends here as you breathe your last, lying on the ground outside the Outlander Club.

THE END

142 "Stop!" a woman's voice rings out loud and clear across the yawning void of the Great Pit of Carkoon, freezing Asajj Ventress where she stands over you, mid attack, ready to finish you with her twin sabers.

You risk a glance in the direction that the voice came from and see a landspeeder come to a stop between the end of the gangplank and Jabba's sail barge. You can hardly believe it when you see that sitting in the back of the speeder, with two clone troopers in attendance, are Master Shaak Ti and Senator Amidala.

You realize that it was the Senator who called a halt to this debacle when she stands to speak.

"Mighty Jabba, I am here on behalf of Chancellor Palpatine and the Galactic Senate to ensure that a grave miscarriage of justice is not carried out. Count Dooku's agents have been playing all of us for fools, trying to sow discontent where there is none and trying to start a war between the Republic and the Hutt clan. Whatever this traitor has told you," she says, pointing at Ventress, "is a lie. We now know that it was your uncle, Ziro the Hutt, who was behind the attack on the Senate on Coruscant, hiring the bounty hunter Vogg Barakk to do his dirty work for him while he is in prison."

On hearing of his uncle's treachery, Jabba mutters something that his protocol droid dares not translate, for fear of offending a Galactic Senator.

You carefully haul yourself back up and, giving Asajj Ventress a wide berth, climb aboard the skiff again.

"It now only remains for me to ask that you allow us to take the Dark Acolyte Asajj Ventress into custody, that she may be tried for her manifold crimes against the Republic and the Jedi Order," the Senator says, concluding her eloquent speech.

Then, before anyone really knows what's going on, Ventress sprints for the end of the gangplank, springs off the end, somersaults through the air, sails over the void between the skiff and the landspeeder, and lands a two-footed kick at the unsuspecting Senator. With a cry of surprise, Padmé Amidala topples over the side of the speeder.

Everyone is so utterly taken by surprise by Ventress's callous act that it is up to you to do something to save the Senator, and you only have a split second in which to act yourself.

If you want to use the Force to save her, turn to page 37.

If you want to leap into the pit after her, turn to page 188.

144 And so it is that you find yourself standing before the main entrance gate to the palace of the notorious crime lord Jabba the Hutt, seeking audience with the mighty Desilijic clan-master himself. You must be mad!

Cautiously you knock on the huge gate, your knocking becoming a resonating clang that echoes away into the vast citadel beyond.

As you wait for a response, a spy-hole opens and the blinking optical receptor of a gatewatcher droid emerges and gives you the once over, making curious burbling, bleeping noises as it does so. You cough politely as the security device looks you up and down before disappearing back into its hole.

For a long time nothing else happens and then, finally, with a great grinding of giant gears, the portcullis grinds open, and you immediately come face-to-face with a pair of brutish, green-skinned Gamorrean Guards. The pug-faced creatures grunt at you whilst waving their vibro-lances menacingly. How will you respond to this threatening behaviour?

If you want to draw your lightsaber and prepare to defend yourself, turn to page 109.

If you want to do nothing in response to the brutish guards' threats, turn to page 77.

145 "You didn't mean to pull out your blaster. You don't know what came over you," you hiss as you focus your mind, making a sweeping gesture as you try to exert your will over the alien.

"I'm sorry, I didn't mean to pull my blaster," the alien says, a confused expression on his face. He lowers his weapon. "I don't know what came over me."

"You're going to put it away now and leave me alone," you mutter, making the hand gesture again.

"I'm going to put it away now and leave you alone," Goshan the Drak says, holstering the blaster and wandering away across the food hall.

The startled onlookers watch him warily as he departs and then slowly return to what they were doing before the incident occurred. A few give you a wide berth from now on, but other than that nothing else untoward happens for the rest of the journey.

Sometime later, the refugee ship drops out of hyperspace and enters the Tatooine system. The planet itself appears as a dusty yellow ball, suspended within the black void of space.

In no time at all it seems, after your long voyage, the vessel is battling the buffeting winds of the planet's atmosphere and coming in to land at one of the planet's largest spaceports – Mos Espa.

Turn to page 35.

146 Having signalled Commander Fox and informed him of your location, you wait in the shelter of an automated smelting plant. You keep the derelict refinery under close observation, until the Coruscant Guard can get there.

And when they do arrive, they arrive in style. Three low-altitude assault infantry transports touch down on the hard standing behind the smeltery, each one carrying a full complement of troopers.

As soon as you are on-board, the gunships lift off again and move on the refinery.

Turn to page 186.

147   "Very well," you agree, "but once this battle is over, nothing changes; we are still sworn enemies, do you understand?"

"As you wish," the assassin says, a sinister smile playing over her lips, and you begin to wonder what you have done.

With the two of you fighting together, side by side, the rancor doesn't stand a chance. In only a matter of moments the beast is dead. Jabba will have to find himself a new pet to entertain him now.

But your victory has come at a price, a price you cannot afford to pay. Having given into your fear of the rancor and your desire for revenge against Jabba the Hutt, you have been betrayed by your darkest emotions. And that means you have given in to the dark side of the Force.

As Ventress climbs on to the back of the fallen rancor, ready to break free of the monster's pit and make her escape, she reaches out her hand to you. You take it, knowing that you have already taken your first step on a path that can only lead to ruin and death, knowing that there is no going back. You have started on the path to the dark side.

You adventure ends here.

THE END

148 The evac alarm wailing from the walls all around you, you turn tail and run. Moving at a sprint you retrace your steps until finally you are hurtling down the steps from the Senate's entrance to the docking platform where the last of the Senatorial escape shuttles are lifting off. But still standing on the landing pad is the Chancellor's personal shuttle, engines powering up, access ramp down, with Shaak Ti and Senator Amidala anxiously hovering before it.

On seeing you, Senator Amidala's face blanches. "Where is the Chancellor?" she asks in a voice that is little more than a shocked whisper.

"I-I don't know," you admit, feeling your face redden in shame as you look from the Senator to your Master and back again. "Isn't he here already?"

"What have you done?" asks Master Ti.

At that moment you are all distracted by the subsonic roar of engines and look up as the hurtling freighter comes into view between the statues of the Republic's founders. You can see it quite clearly now as it makes its final terrible approach on the Senate. Everyone runs for the shuttle.

And then, suddenly, the vessel alters its trajectory, rising sharply, and the plummeting freighter clears the Senate. The subsonic thrumming of its engines nearly shakes you off your feet, but at least you are still alive.

"The Senate is safe!" you gasp in relief, as fire-suppression ships guide the freighter towards a safe landing site.

"No thanks to you," says Master Ti disparagingly. "We have Trin'dal Vek to thank for that."

There is a commotion behind you and Chancellor Palpatine emerges from the Senate building accompanied by his personal retinue. But even the sight of the Chancellor alive and well does nothing to soften the expression of disgust etched on to the Togruta's face.

"You put your life above that of the Chancellor and thereby the future of the entire Republic!" she hisses with barely contained rage.

You have never seen Master Ti like this. You wish the Sarlacc of Tatooine would swallow you up right there and then.

"You obviously do not have what it takes to become a true Jedi. I hereby dismiss you from the Order forthwith. Give me your lightsaber."

Slowly, in a state of shock, you remove your lightsaber from the belt of your robe and place it into Master Ti's open hand. "Never darken the door of the Temple again," is the last thing she says to you, before she turns on her heel and strides away to consult with Commander Fox again.

You are left feeling hollow and empty. But it is your own selfish behaviour that has brought you to this point, cast out of the Jedi Order. All your hopes for a glorious future as a Jedi Knight of the Galactic Republic have been dashed. Your adventure is over.

THE END

150 You waste precious moments waiting while the droid disengages itself from its emplacement within the wing of the starfighter until finally it is free.

Then, anxious to be off, with R2-X4 trundling after you, you set off for the freighter's flight deck as fast as you can.

Turn to page 20.

151 The Gamorreans lead you to a large barred door, heave it open and then shove you into the darkness beyond.

As your eyes become accustomed to the gloom, you find yourself inside a pit dug out of the bedrock beneath the palace. The deeply gouged scratch marks of something large, with equally large claws, cover the walls while bones litter the floor of the pit, some human, some alien, and some belonging to much larger creatures. You dread to think what it is that calls this place home.

With a tortured creaking and groaning, a scarred gate on the other side of the cave-pit starts to rise and you hear the snuffling of some large beast coming from behind it. A huge claw slips through the widening gap and grasps the bottom of the gate, helping to push it up into the groove in the rock above. With an enraged roar, a fully-grown rancor enters the pit.

The monster stands five metres tall and is just as broad, with a flat blunt head, large fanged maw dripping with digestive spittle, and long grasping claws. The prospect of taking on such a monstrous opponent armed with only your lightsaber would be intimidating enough, but without your lightsaber, what can you do to defend yourself?

It is just as you are wondering how you are ever going to get yourself out of such a dire predicament that you hear the shouts and jeers coming from up above. Light spills into the pit through a grille in the roof of the cave and beyond that you can make out the crime lord

Jabba the Hutt and his court, as they, in turn, peer down at you, ready to savour the spectacle of the inevitable slaughter to come.

The chorus of whistles and cat-calls from the watching aliens only makes you all the more determined not to give them what they want and thwart their expectations of the entertainment to come.

If you want to run from the rancor, by escaping through the gateway by which it entered the pit, turn to page 183.

If you want to charge straight at the rancor, despite the obvious danger, click box K on screen and type code word RANCOR or turn to page 165.

153 Pushing the pedal to the floor, you bravely – or should that be recklessly? – steer the landspeeder straight towards the krayt dragon. The already battered vehicle slams into one of the monster's colossal legs but it is you who comes off worse from the collision.

It is as if you have driven into a solid wall of stone. The creature roars in pain but it barely moves at all, whereas you are thrown clear of the landspeeder to land sprawled in the sand at the monster's feet, under its gaping mouth.

All it takes is one sharp snap of the dragon's jaws and your adventure comes to an abrupt and gruesome end as a light snack for a krayt dragon.

THE END

154 Despite the pressing nature of your mission, you skid to a halt to hear what the clone trooper has to report.

"If you're looking for the Chancellor," he says, "you should know that the Senate was not in session when the command to evacuate was given."

Thanking the clone for this information, you push into the building in the face of the crush of fleeing beings.

If the Senate is not in session, the most likely place you would expect to find Chancellor Palpatine would be in his suite of private offices.

Turn to page 78.

155 Long range scans suggest that you will be able to take the LAAT/is around the decayed zone and cut the bounty hunter off on the other side, when he tries to leave again. You suggest this strategy to Commander Fox.

"That sounds like a plan to me, Padawan," the commander agrees. And so the three gunships give the impression of breaking off from their pursuit of the Snivvian bounty hunter and set off on a different heading to circumnavigate the industrialized no man's land.

The squadron is coming in low under a series of crane gantries when something colossal lurches into the path of the gunships.

You barely have time to register that it is a gigantic lifter droid, which has gone rogue after years of neglect, its central processing unit having malfunctioned long ago.

The monstrous droid gives a grinding mechanical roar as it lumbers towards the gunships, making a grab for the closest LAAT/i with huge lifter arms that once carried sections of planetary assault ship fuselages around the factory works.

If you think you should target the droid with the gunship's weapons, click box N on screen and type code word FIRE, or turn to page 129.

If you would rather tell the squadron to scramble and get out of the way as quickly as possible to avoid any contact with the rogue droid, turn to page 94.

156 In a blur of movement your lightsaber is in your hands, the rod of blue light humming as you bring it to bear.

Suddenly a series of detonations peppers the hangar, as someone – or some*thing* – opens fire on the Toydarian's business premises. Windows shatter and holes are punched in the metal skin of the building by searing laser fire.

Creating sweeping arcs in front of you with your whirling lightsaber, you defend yourself, repelling as many of the laser blasts as you can, but you are no Anakin Skywalker and you cannot hold off against all of them. Several laser blasts hit you and you drop to the floor of the hangar on your knees.

Gasping from the pain, you are still conscious when the assassin droid enters the hangar. It regards you with a pulsing red photoreceptor, emitting a series of whirring hums as it registers the threat level you present. Then it identifies the lightsaber still in your hands and opens fire again!

KAPOW! Your adventure is over.

THE END

157 Bringing the starfighter around again you lock on to the cargo bay doors this time and direct a second volley of laser fire at the freighter. The laser cannons punch through the metal doors and you fly the starfighter straight into the cargo hold.

Not concerned with trying to land your craft carefully, you put the starfighter down as quickly as you can and, releasing the cockpit canopy, leap out before it has even finished sliding to a halt.

It could be only a matter of minutes now before the freighter reaches the Senate. There's no time to lose, so without further delay you set off for the flight deck.

Turn to page 20.

158 You catch Ventress out completely as you run into her next twin-bladed attack and, as you parry the crimson sabers, you vault over the Dark Acolyte completely. You land on both feet at the other end of the gangplank, within reach of the sand skiff itself.

As you turn, ready to make full use of the advantage you think you have gained, you are met by a vicious kick that sends you sprawling on to the plank on your back. For a moment you are left completely exposed and open to attack, as you struggle to bring your lightsaber to bear before Ventress can land a killing blow, but you are not quick enough.

Turn to page 142.

160 Eager to be off, not sure what else might be lurking in the stinking rubbish marshes and certainly not wanting to run into any carnivorous denizens of the swamp, you set out. Bounding from one bobbing mat of weed to the next, you keep an eye out just in case and tune into the background chorus of unsettling croaks and chirrups, listening for any change in pitch or rhythm that might indicate that you are in danger.

When the attack comes, however, it is a complete surprise. A knotty tentacle slips out of the swamp, wrapping around your ankle and giving a sharp tug. You are pulled from your feet and land badly. Frantically you make a grab for the floating weed mat as the tentacle starts to pull you into the black waters of the rubbish swamp.

As you grab at the thick ropes of weed with one hand, with the other you reach for your lightsaber. It is then that you see a watery eye on a veiny stalk rise out of the swamp in front of you. The eye blinks at you myopically. You have fallen foul of a dianoga, a horror also known as a rubbish squid.

You hack at the beast with your lightsaber, trying to cut through the eye-stalk as the dianoga reaches for you with even more of its rubbery tentacles, one almost managing to worm its way around your neck.

And then, just when the battle is at its most vicious, the swamp becomes awash with light and sound, the thrumming of repulsor jets beating the water into waves all around you. The monstrous squid makes one last feeble attempt to drag you into its gaping, fang-lined maw and you respond by slicing your lightsaber through one of its writhing tentacle limbs. And then it is gone, disappearing back beneath the oily waters, in search of easier prey.

You struggle back on to the weed mat gasping for breath, as a clone trooper drops on to the spongy carpet on the end of a descent line, suspended from a LAAT/i gunship hovering overhead.

"Come with me," he says, offering you his hand.

In a few minutes you are recovering on-board the Republic gunship as it, and two others, with a full complement of clone troopers each, sets off for the Works district – the place they managed to track the assassin droid to on its return flight.

Three gunships, you think. Commander Fox obviously isn't taking any chances.

Turn to page 186.

162 "I need to see Dexter Jettster and I need to see him now," you tell the droid waitress, whose designation you see is WA-7.

She immediately comes back at you with, "Well is that right? Dexter's real busy right now. It's the lunchtime rush, you see? Wouldn't you rather come back later?"

"No," you snarl in annoyance, "it's alright. I'll wait."

And wait you do. A few minutes later WA-7 returns to the stall you have taken by the window with a menu in her robotic hand but you wave her away irritably.

An hour passes and there's still no sign that you're going to get the chance to speak to the Besalisk anytime soon. You can't help thinking that the longer you delay here, the more time the villain behind the attack on the Senate has to make his getaway — even get offworld.

If you want to keep waiting to see Dexter, turn to page 131.

If you decide not to waste anymore time here when there's a villain to catch, turn to page 55.

163 You decide not to take any chances and make preparations to travel to Tatooine in disguise, boarding a refugee ship that is carrying people from Coruscant to the planets of the Outer Rim, and away from the frontline of the war between the Republic and the Confederacy of Independent Systems that has divided the galaxy.

During the long voyage to the desert world of Tatooine you take time to recuperate from the stresses and strains of your recent adventures. You also practice your lightsaber skills and test your athletic agility, as well as communing with the Force to hone the mind skills taught to you during long hours of training at the Jedi Temple on Coruscant.

There are all sorts of alien species on-board the refugee ship, seeking somewhere safe to wait out the war. One distinctive-looking passenger stands out in particular. His skin is blue and his long face is bisected by a knotty red scar.

If the name, Goshan the Drak, means anything to you, turn to page 36.

If you have never heard the name before, turn to page 125.

164 Bowing your head you make your heart-felt plea. "But, Master, do we not learn from our mistakes?" you begin. "Indeed, do we not learn more through them than we do through all the hours we might undertake in training at the Temple?"

The Jedi listens with interest as you put forward your case. "Go on."

"I made a mistake, I admit that. I have fallen short of what is required of me as a Jedi. But when we fall we must ask ourselves why, and I believe the answer is so that we can learn to pick ourselves up again. I have fallen," you say, "I have picked myself up again, and now I humbly beseech you to give me another chance, Master Ti."

The Jedi regards you for a moment more, an inscrutable expression on her face. And then she says simply, "Very well. You have won your appeal. You have one more chance to prove yourself worthy of the title of Jedi."

You feel giddy with delight but remind yourself to be calm; you don't want to mess things up now.

Turn to page 103.

165 Taking your courage, and your life, in both hands, you run straight at the monstrous beast, even as it lunges forward to grasp you in its cruel meat-hook claws as it locates you at last. But the rancor's claws close on nothing but empty air as, at the last possible moment, you launch yourself into the air in a death-defying somersault.

You land on the monster's arm and scramble up to its shoulder. From the rancor's arching back you throw yourself at the grille above you.

Grabbing hold of a metal strut with one hand, you pull yourself up far enough to poke your head and an arm through one of the holes in the grille. From there it's only a matter of stretching out your hand for your lightsaber – that is currently in the possession of the Gamorrean guard that took it from you – and summoning your weapon to you with your mind. The lightsaber hits your hand and, its blue blade igniting again, you cut yourself free.

You pull yourself to your feet, panting for breath, in the middle of Jabba the Hutt's throne room. A tense, nervous hush descends over the crime lord's court as a cloaked figure steps clear of the huddle of wary aliens, throwing back the hood of her cloak as she does so. Seeing the hairless head revealed beneath, your blood runs cold.

Standing at the other end of the raised dais on which the slug-like Jabba sits is the sworn enemy of the Jedi, and agent of Count Dooku, Asajj Ventress herself!

Turn to page 123.

167 The Klatooinian enforcers take you into custody, securing you within a cage cell, and it takes some time for you to persuade the duty officer to contact the Coruscant Guard on your behalf.

It is blushing with shame and embarrassment that you have to face the clone trooper contingent that Commander Fox sends to secure your release and you're sure the clones must be laughing at you behind your back.

And so it is that you finally join Commander Fox and his clone troopers as they head off deeper into the underlevels of the world-city.

Turn to page 23.

168 You leap forward with a shout born of wrath and the need for vengeance, but, no matter how spirited and well-intentioned your attack might be, it leaves you exposed.

Ventress sweeps in under your guard with both her blazing lightsabers. You manage to parry one, but not the other. The crimson blade slices through your body. Losing your balance as you blackout from the pain, you slip from the side of the narrow gangplank and plummet into the Great Pit of Carkoon, where the snapping tongue of the hungry Sarlacc is waiting for you.

You end your adventure here, as supper for the Sarlacc.

THE END

169 Steering the landspeeder towards the dragon, at the last possible moment, as the monster lunges for you with its huge fang-filled jaws, you leap clear of the speeder, your lightsaber humming into life as you do so.

You swing your weapon to left and right as you somersault over the dragon's head and land in the sand on both feet, lightsaber at the ready again. A moment later, the reptile's huge head drops on to the dunes behind you, your unstoppable energy blade having cut through its neck completely.

The threat passed, you recover your landspeeder from where it has ploughed into a sand dune, and set off again for Jabba's Palace.

Click box I on screen and type code word PALACE or turn to page 180.

170 You enter the turbo-lift and ride it to the Chancellor's office. You emerge into a suite of rooms totally devoid of life, apart from one man.

As you enter, a guard wearing a crimson cloak and a featureless helm, and bearing a potentially lethal force pike in his hands, whirls round to face you.

"What are you doing here?" demands the Red Guard. This man is one of the Chancellor's elite protectors and not to be messed with.

You introduce yourself. "I am Padawan to Master Shaak Ti of the Jedi Temple," you say, staring up into the blank helm-mask of the imposing red-robed figure. "I am here to make sure the Chancellor gets to safety."

"The Chancellor and his retinue have already been evacuated," he informs you, his tone as cold as the ice-world of Hoth. "And it's time we got out of here too. Now move!"

You realize that there is no point in arguing with the resolute guard and so do as he says.

Turn to page 127.

171 In one fluid action you whip out your lightsaber, activate the energy beam and use it to slice your aggressor's blaster in two.

The shocked alien drops the now useless weapon and throws up his hands in surrender. "I give up!" he yelps, but you do not let your guard down until two of the ship's security officers turn up to take the desperado away with them, to make him secure for the rest of the journey to Tatooine.

But your dealing with the notorious death stick dealer, Goshan the Drak, has not gone unnoticed and your cover is blown. Everyone onboard now knows that you are a Jedi in training. And the news travels around the whole ship faster than a case of Corellian mumps.

Turn to page 135.

172 Holding tight to the edge of the hole you cut for yourself in the trapdoor, you reach down to the cornered Ventress. A sinister smile turns the corners of her mouth as you do so.

In a series of incredible, death-defying leaps and bounds, she somersaults over the advancing rancor, landing on its back, and from there launches herself up to you, only just managing to catch hold of your outstretched hand.

"My thanks, Jedi," she gasps as you pull her up and out of the pit. "Now if I were you, I'd run for it."

The croaking cry of the enraged Jabba and the hoots and screams of his various hangers-on crashes against you in a wave of sound. You and your Dark Acolyte ally have managed to make yourselves the most unpopular people on Tatooine as far as Jabba the Hutt is concerned. You have no choice but to flee.

As you run from the palace, after the fleeing Ventress, you know that Jabba will send mercenaries and bounty hunters to hunt you down and make you pay for the way you have insulted him. At the same time, you realize that you have betrayed the trust that Master Ti and the Jedi Council placed in you. There can be no place for you within the Jedi Order anymore. As that horribly cruel realization dawns, Asajj Ventress looks back at you with that same sinister smile on her lips.

"Come with me!" she says, and as you reach for her outstretched hand this time you realize that there is no hope for you now. After all, by helping Ventress in the first place, you have already taken your first step on the path to becoming one with the dark side of the Force.

Your adventure, just like your future as a true Jedi knight, is over.

THE END

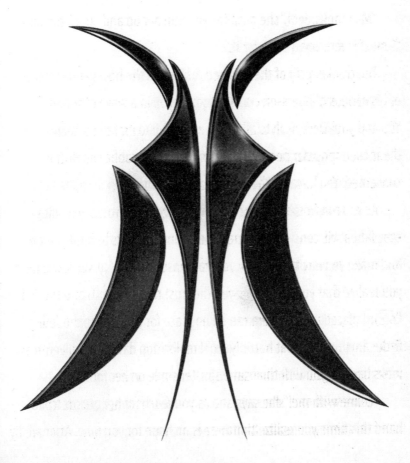

174 Jabba the Hutt? You can hardly believe what you are hearing. You know that the Hutts are gangsters who control trade routes throughout the Outer Rim but you had thought that Jabba himself was an ally of the Republic. Since Anakin Skywalker and his Padawan, Ahsoka Tano, rescued his kidnapped son Rotta the Huttlet from his Separatist kidnappers, he has allowed the clone armies of the Republic to use his space-lanes to transport troops throughout the galaxy. Why would he turn on the Republic now, even going so far as to have Chancellor Palpatine assassinated?

You tell Master Ti all this when you deliver the bounty hunter into her custody and take the opportunity to voice your concerns.

"It is a mystery indeed," she agrees, "and I believe there is more to this than it would first appear." She keeps her own counsel for a moment. Then she says, "We need to find out the truth of Jabba's plans. I want you to travel to Tatooine. Find out as much as you can. I will remain here on Coruscant and see what I can find out from this end. Remember to watch your back. If this is a Separatist ploy, nothing but danger could await you on Tatooine."

Your chest swells with pride. Danger may well await you on the distant backwater dustball world of Tatooine but Shaak Ti thinks you are capable of handling such an important mission on your own. It's now up to you to decide how best to pursue your investigation. If Jabba the Hutt is behind the attack on the Senate you might do well to travel to Tatooine in secret. But then, if this *is* all part of a Separatist plot to engineer a war between the Hutts and the Republic, then perhaps it would be best to meet with Jabba face to face.

If you want to travel to Tatooine in secret, turn to page 163.

If you want to travel to Tatooine openly, as a representative of the Jedi Order, to seek an audience with Jabba the Hutt, turn to page 74.

176 "I request the right of trial by combat!" you declare for all to hear. The slug-like Hutt looks at you quizzically and then speaks.

"The mighty Jabba wishes to know against whom it is you wish to fight," TC-70 translates.

"Against the one who has made these outrageous claims against the Jedi Order."

The Hutt puts a fat hand to his wobbly chin and considers your proposal for several long seconds.

If you travelled to Tatooine on-board a Jedi starfighter, turn to page 33.

If not, turn to page 59.

177 To leave yourself unarmed, with your mortal enemy stalking towards you whilst holding two lightsabers, seems like utter madness. But then your fingertips slip again and you are left dangling from the gangplank, with all your weight supported by only your middle finger – and it isn't enough.

Unable to hold on any longer, the gangplank slips away from you and you plunge into the dreaded Pit of Carkoon, there to be devoured by the Sarlacc, very slowly! It will take 1,000 years for the creature to digest you completely.

Your adventure ends here with you suffering a most grisly fate.

THE END

178 Without the aid of a droid and its ability to perform a million combinations a second you have to resort to using your Jedi powers to help you crack the code.

Focusing on the navicom, you try to see beyond the glowing green numbers of the digital display to the memory core and the hiding place of the encrypted code that will unlock the computer.

And then you have it. In your mind you see the digital display, now reading the correct series of digits. There is a sharp click and a bleep as the autopilot disengages, and excited relief rushes through you.

Turn to page 110.

179 Not taking your eyes off Jabba's monstrous pet, not for a moment, you call out to the Dark Acolyte. "Say what you have to say, Ventress, and be quick about it!"

"The Hutt has played us both false," she says, "and if either of us wants to get out of here alive, we are going to have to work together to defeat this monster."

One minute she's making out that you're an assassin sent to murder Jabba, the next she's suggesting you work together against the alien gangster.

"So, what do you say?" the Dark Acolyte asks. "Are you with me?"

The ravening monster is almost on top of you. Whatever you are going to do, you need to decide quickly!

If you agree to join with Ventress to defeat the rancor, turn to page 147.

If you would rather lay down your life than aid a sworn enemy of the Jedi, turn to page 44.

180 And then at last, after surviving such a perilous trek across the Tatooine wilderness, the imposing fortress, that is now the lair of one of the most feared creatures in the galaxy, comes into view amidst the rocky uplands at the edge of the Northern Dune Sea.

Just the sight of the place fills you with trepidation. You have the feeling that your mission is almost at an end. Perhaps your heightened Jedi senses are the reason you believe the answers you seek, as to the truth of what happened on Coruscant, with the audacious attack on the Galactic Senate, will be revealed within.

But now that you have finally reached your goal, how will you go about uncovering the truth?

If you want to approach the front gate and request an audience with his eminence Jabba the Hutt, turn to page 144.

If you would prefer to enter the gangster's lair surreptitiously, turn to 88.

181 Scanning an eye over the menu being proffered you by the droid waitress, whose designation you see is WA-7, you settle for an Aitha protein drink politely adding, "Is there any chance I could have a word with Dexter when he gets a minute?"

"One Aitha it is," WA-7 says, repeating your order. "I'll see if Dexter's free but I have to warn you, we're real busy right now, OK?"

You take a look around the diner. The droid's not wrong. You see grumbling Dugs sitting alongside hungry Nuknogs, while a party of Rodians crowd the stalls at the far end of the bar.

"It's OK, I'll wait," you say, taking a seat at the bar next to an ugly looking Gran from the planet Hok.

And wait you do. After a few minutes the droid waitress returns with your drink but half an hour later you're still waiting for a chance to speak to Dexter. An hour and two more Aithas later, and the Besalisk still looks like he's going to be stuck in the kitchen for the foreseeable future.

"Whatever it is you want to talk to the Besalisk about, it must be pretty important, Jedi," a reptilian creature growls from the other side of the bar.

Turning, you stiffen, as you see that it is the notorious Trandoshan scavenger Gha Nachkt speaking. The reptilian alien fixes you with a twinkling stare and scratches his chin with a scaly claw. "If your galactic credits are good, maybe I could help."

Dealing with a low-life junk ghoul like Gha Nachkt isn't the sort of thing you'd normally consider doing, but time is pressing and Dexter seems otherwise occupied.

If you want to pay Gha Nachkt for any information he might have, click on box C and type the code word NACHKT, or turn to page 62.

If you decide that you don't want to waste any more time waiting here when there's a villain to catch, turn to page 55.

183 Seeing how the monster is swaying its head from side to side, you realize that it hasn't actually seen you yet. Its tiny eyes being next to useless, it is trying to sniff you out instead.

Seizing the opportunity, you sprint past the rancor and under the portcullis, and run right into the monster's den. The smell of rotting meat lingers unpleasantly in the air around you. Half-chewed bones litter the floor while the walls here have been gouged by the monster's claws as well, as it rages against its captivity. Sadly there is not another way out.

The rancor's den is a dead-end, quite literally as far as you are concerned. Understanding the terrible mistake you have made, you slowly turn to face the savage beast that has found your scent at last. With the rancor blocking the only way out, there's no escaping it this time. Your adventure ends here, as a tasty snack for Jabba's monstrous pet.

THE END

184 Keeping their blasters and vibro-lances trained on you, just in case you should try anything foolish, your guards release you from your bonds and, once you are back at the far end of the gangplank, toss you your lightsaber. You deftly snatch it out of the air as the Dark Acolyte somersaults across the space between the sail barge and the skiff, and lands at the other end of the gangplank.

As she lights her twin sabers you consider, really for the first time, how you are going to best a mistress of the dark side of the Force who has survived encounters with both Master Obi-Wan Kenobi and Anakin Skywalker.

"This should be fun," Ventress says with a sneer, swinging her crimson blades around her in a dextrous display of martial skill.

If you want to seize the initiative and leap forward to attack, turn to page 168.

If you want to prepare to defend yourself, turn to page 93.

186 You now know who tried to wipe out the Galactic Senate on Coruscant. The villain you are stalking is the scrupleless Snivvian bounty hunter Vogg Barakk, who is hiding out within the lawless industrialized Works district.

It is a place of abandoned self-maintaining factories, uncontrolled power surges and the favoured refuge of many a smuggler gang. Under an oppressive crimson sky, Commander Fox's hunting party enters the Works. The sight of three Republic gunships flying in over the shell of warehouses and factory barns in attack formation is an impressive thing indeed, designed to strike fear into the forces of the Confederacy of Independent Systems on a battlefield. Many times a Separatist army has turned tail and run on seeing the elite forces of the Republic's clone armies, led by their Jedi generals, hove into view over the horizon being carried by a fleet of LAAT/i gunships and trundling juggernauts. You can imagine the kind of impression it would make on the sort of low-life scum you are now hunting.

Each Low-Altitude Assault Transport is carrying a full complement of clone troopers. On-board the lead vessel are both Commander Fox and yourself. The commander obviously doesn't want the prey to get away.

As you are closing on the abandoned carbonite refinery in which Vogg Barakk has his hideout, the Snivvian takes flight – quite literally – making a break for it in a heavily-armed Techno Union-style starfighter.

"Don't let him get away," Fox orders the pilot of your gunship and, signalling the rest of the attack party, sets off in pursuit.

Knowing that if he leaves the cover of the industrial zone the gunships will be all over him like an Elomin rash, the bounty hunter leads your LAAT/is further into the lawless mechanized tracts and power conduit canyons formed by the disused factories and automated power stations of the Works.

It soon becomes clear that Vogg Barakk hopes to lose you within a particularly decayed region of the Works that looks like it has been left derelict for centuries. Some of the buildings here have already toppled into one another while giant rusted derricks stand watch like crumbling sentinels.

Commander Fox seems determined to follow the bounty hunter into this dead zone, no matter what.

If you are happy with this course of action, turn to page 67.

If you think the bounty hunter is leading you into a trap and you want to suggest a different approach, turn to page 155.

188 Your heightened Jedi reactions are so fast that you are already running for the gangplank as Padmé begins to fall over the side of the landspeeder, a grapple gun you found lying in the bottom of the sand skiff clasped tightly in your hands.

You leap into the pit as you fire the grappling gun at the side of the hovering speeder. As the grapple claw anchors itself to the side of the vessel, the cable pulls tight against the gun in your hands and you swing round in a great arc underneath the landspeeder, intercepting Padmé's fall at the bottom of your swing.

You are left dangling over the Great Pit of Carkoon above the gaping maw of the Sarlacc, as you wait for Master Ti and the clones to haul you and Padmé to safety, but at least Senator Amidala is safe.

Hearing shouts from the skiff, you look up to see Asajj Ventress dispatch the last of Jabba's guards with her lethal crimson sabers, take hold of the sand skiff's controls and then pilot it away over the rippling dunes of the desert, the Dark Acolyte making her escape
in the end.

Ventress may have lived to fight another day and escaped capture once again but you can feel proud nonetheless. Senator Amidala is safe, you have proved yourself as a Jedi and you have played no small part in diffusing the crisis that began on Coruscant.

You can return to Coruscant and the Jedi Temple secure in the knowledge that thanks to you, war between the Republic and the Hutts has been averted and that today, you are the hero!

THE END